The Great Laundry Adventure

The Great Laundry Adventure

by Margie Rutledge

illustrations by Maxine Cowan

Napoleon Publishing

Cover art: Chrissie Wysotski

Le Conseil des Arts du Canada DEPUIS 1957 | The Canada Council FOR THE ARTS SINCE 1957

Napoleon gratefully acknowledges the support of the
Canada Council for the Arts for our publishing program.

Napoleon Publishing
Toronto, Ontario, Canada

Printed in Canada

05 04 03 02 01 00 99   5 4 3 2 1

Canadian Cataloguing in Publication Data

Rutledge, Margie, date

ISBN 0-929141-67-9

I. Cowan, Maxine, date.   II. Title.

PS8585.U864G73 1999   jC81'.54   C99-931192-1
PZ7.R938G73   1999

For my parents
and
for E, J, V and B
with love.

Acknowledgments

Little Star by Aline Rutledge
A Card Game in the Dark by Espe Currie
Roncesvalles Lovers by Margie Rutledge
The Ballad of the Spanish Civil Guard (excerpt)
by Federico Garcia Lorca, translated by A. L. Lloyd from
The Selected Poems of Federico Garcia Lorca, copyright©1955
by New Directions Publishing Corp.
Reprinted by permission of New Directions Publishing Corp.

Chapter One

The Beginning: A Solution

Abigail, Jacob and Ernest lived in a house without closets. It was an old house: older than your mother or your grandmother or even your great-grandmother. The hallways were excellent for sock-skating, and they joined together rather like a maze (except without closets, there weren't so many dead ends).

It was a house the children spent a lot of time in because, like many modern children, Abigail, Jacob and Ernest were not free. They did not explore the streets and alleys and ravines looking for adventure. Their outings to High Park or the waterfront or along the Humber River (for our children lived in Toronto) were always with an adult who never let them out of sight. And it was a bother always to be in sight, a bother to the children and a bother to their parents. In warm weather, they played in the back garden, but city gardens rarely have the secret places children most enjoy.

It was lucky that the children had a big, untidy house in which to play, and it was even luckier the children had large, unruly imaginations.

At the time of this story, Abigail was ten years old and the eldest of the three. By the time this story was over, Abigail had grown up a lot very quickly, but that's jumping ahead. In any case, like both her brothers, Abigail had clear blue eyes. She had beautiful waist-length wavy brown hair and though she could have been very vain about it, she thought of it mostly as a nuisance and often pleaded with her mother to cut it. Her mother resisted because the hair made Abigail look special, as if she were not entirely of her own time.

Jacob, who was seven, had been very blond as a baby, but his hair had darkened somewhat. On first impression, he seemed older than his years, but he had been that way since he was an infant. His height and slenderness, along with the paleness of his complexion, gave him a frail quality, though he was actually quite athletic.

Ernest was four and something of a perpetual motion machine. He was between Abigail and Jacob in colouring and had the same blue eyes. He loved to talk, and his family could always track his location in that big house by the sound of his voice. He talked himself into wakefulness in the morning, talked and muttered through the day and then talked himself to sleep again at night.

But back to the house without closets, for the lack of closets posed a problem for the Lawrence family.

This problem was made worse by the fact that no one in the family had a chest of drawers that worked. Drawers got stuck, or the knobs fell off, and why struggle to put clothes in if you were so soon to take them out again?

Most clothes were kept in the parents' bedroom: a room with eleven walls (Jacob liked to count them) painted Cleopatra blue. One rarely noticed the Cleopatraness though, because on one side of the room was a four-foot high pile of clean clothes and on the other side of the room was a four-foot high pile of dirty clothes.

Every morning when the children had to get dressed, they would dive into the pile of clean clothes and thrash about until they found socks, a pair of underwear, a shirt and maybe jeans or overalls. No one ever found a *pair* of socks, and it was a family belief that only nerds wore matching socks. Some mornings the search for clothes was an adventure, and on other mornings it was a catastrophe. The worst days were when the pile of clean clothes would get mixed up with the pile of dirty clothes, and the children's mother would insist on inspecting everything because she didn't want her children going out of the house in dirty clothes.

"Disorganization is one thing, but slovenliness is quite

another," she would say while spit-cleaning spaghetti sauce off a shirt sleeve and then handing it to a child. After a momentary burst of attention to domestic detail, the mother would invariably drift downstairs to the piano and play The Queen of the Night's aria over and over and over. She loved her children very much, but she was a little dreamy.

If the mother was a little dreamy, the father was a man of action, albeit a crusty man of action. For a number of years the laundry situation had bothered him, and for a few years after that, it had troubled him. He was on the verge of real annoyance on the morning he almost had to borrow Jacob's Boston Bruins sweater (which was about eighteen sizes too small) because he couldn't unearth a clean sweater of his own.

"This is madness," Jacob said to Abigail when he saw his father measuring the sweater across his chest. And the father had to agree. There had to be a solution. It was fortunate for the family that Abigail, Jacob and Ernest were imaginative and competent beyond their years.

"Ali Baba and the Forty Thieves!" announced Abigail.

"Huh?" Jacob responded.

"You know—jars full of treasure and jewels and olive oil," said Abigail.

"Yeah, olive oil," Ernest agreed.

Jacob, who was sometimes very literal-minded, asked: "You think we should wear olive oil instead of clothes?"

"No, no, no, no," insisted Abigail. "The jars!"

"What about the jars?"

Abigail let out a deep and impatient sigh. "Don't you get it?"

"Get what? Am I supposed to read your mind?"

"Jacob, you are such a boy sometimes. If I live to be a hundred, I will never understand boys."

"And if I live to be two thousand years old, I'll never understand girls."

"There's a lot you wouldn't understand in two thousand years."

"Dad!" cried Jacob.

But the father didn't hear because he was burrowing into another pile of laundry in search of a sweater he could actually wear.

"Mom, Abigail's being mean to me again!"

But the mother didn't hear because this morning she was in the bathroom looking in the mirror, trying to figure out how much she had aged in the last week.

"Listen, remember those giant jars the forty thieves hid in?" asked Abigail.

"They all got killed," said Jacob.

"That wouldn't happen to us. We live in Toronto and we don't even hang out with criminals," Abigail assured her brothers.

"The criminals could keep it secret," said Ernest.

"Keep what secret?" asked Abigail.

"That they *are* criminals," said Ernest.

"Forget the criminals. We're talking about laundry," said Abigail.

"Besides which, we can hardly even cross the street without Mommy and Daddy, so I don't know where we'd meet people dangerous enough or diabolical enough to do us in like the forty thieves," rationalized Jacob.

"As to the issue at hand," Abigail began, "we could put laundry instead of treasure in some giant jars. Not only would things be a little better organized, but we'd have a place to hide. Children with closets have places to hide. I've done it at other people's houses and it's really fun."

"I want to hide, I really want to hide," said Ernest, as he jumped up and down on a pile of laundry not containing his father.

"I don't know where we're going to get the jars. As far as I know, there are no magic caves around here," complained Jacob.

"High Park is sure to have some magic caves," suggested Ernest.

"I've never seen them," said Jacob.

"If we can't get jars, then we need giant somethingorothers," insisted Abigail.

"Bachas," their father gasped, as he surfaced from his dive, a navy blue extra large sweater clutched in one hand.

"Huh?" the children said in unison.

"Baskets. I knew I'd come up with a solution. We'll go down to Spadina on Saturday and buy as many baskets as we can fit in the car. The Lawrence family will not be defeated by laundry. We will have order in our lives!"

The children were late for school that day, but they had hope in their hearts: their lives were going to change somehow.

※ ※ ※

The following Saturday, the family drove down to Spadina Avenue to buy baskets. The parents were a little dazed as to where to begin; the mother (who did all the driving) had refused to go into a parkade and had driven up and down the streets of Kensington Market for forty minutes looking for a parking spot. Jacob finally found one tucked between crates of pigeons on one end and dried cod on the other. The

mother miraculously managed to parallel park without flattening anything or anybody.

"Now stay together! I don't want to lose anybody," ordered their father as they all piled out of the car. "Ernest, stay with me!"

But Ernest was nowhere to be seen.

"Ernest? Ernest!" and then finally, "ERNEST!" screamed their mother, who had long ago lost any self-consciousness about yelling in public.

It seemed as if every creature within a six-block radius turned to stare at the family, and Saturday morning at Kensington Market included a lot of creatures: humans (of course) and dogs and cats and chickens and every other kind of fowl and rabbits and rodents and seafood with great buggy eyes and even a few monkeys. Abigail and Jacob had the feeling that some of the fruits and vegetables were also looking at the family curiously after their mother yelled for Ernest.

As it turned out, Ernest had simply spotted a monkey and followed it down a dark alley. He knew, absolutely, this was something he shouldn't do, but he couldn't help himself. The monkey chattered at him, and as Ernest listened, it seemed as if the monkey was speaking a language Ernest could understand. Ernest's concentration was abruptly fractured by his mother's hullabaloo, and he followed its echo back to his family.

"Ernest, sweetie!" cried his mother as she scooped him up in her arms.

"Don't you ever..." began his father.

After the reprimand, Ernest told his family that he'd found a shop selling baskets—they just had to follow the monkey. Sure enough, when they looked over to where Ernest pointed, a tiny grey and black monkey with a long tail (the kind of monkey organ grinders used to use) stood waiting for them. Ernest and the monkey led the way and the parents followed. Abigail and Jacob brought up the rear.

"Do you ever think sometimes they're not quite sure what they're doing?" asked Abigail.

"You mean Mommy and Daddy?" asked Jacob.

"Yeah," said Abigail.

"Yeah, I do," said Jacob.

The two were quiet for a moment.

"Maybe it's just being a grown-up," Jacob said, wanting to believe the best.

"No. It's them," asserted Abigail with conviction. "They seem so nervous and frightened all the time."

"Daddy's not that nervous," said Jacob.

"He's nervous about us," said Abigail. "They both are. They're scared that something's going to happen. I mean, don't you think it's peculiar that kids always *want* something to happen, and parents are scared that something actually *will?*"

And there the conversation ended because the family found themselves in an unnaturally darkened alley in front of a door hung with layers of beaded curtains.

"This certainly is exotic," said the mother.

"I'm not even sure it's a store," said the father.

"It is," said Ernest as he and the monkey separated the lines of beads and passed through. The other members of the family simply followed.

The interior was completely dark except for Christmas lights draped in waves across the ceiling. It took a few minutes for everyone to accustom themselves to the room. As their eyes travelled from the ceiling down, the family saw richly embroidered kimonos and shawls hung along the walls, shelves crowded with buddhas in all sizes and colours, teapots and woks and mysterious cooking utensils all jammed together in a corner and baskets of every size and shape and colour ajumble in one section of the room.

Only after they had a clear sense of the merchandise did they spot the shopkeeper, a plump little old woman with hair the colour of strawberries and very blue eyelids. Later the children noticed that her eyes were green, but then the red hair and blue makeup were so bright, even in the semi-darkness, that everyone was shocked they hadn't seen the woman right away.

"You met my monkey," said the woman in a smoky, old-fashioned movie star kind of voice.

"Yes, we need some laundry baskets," explained the mother.

"I have just the thing," the woman said and moved over to the baskets to help the mother and father choose the ones they wanted.

Abigail and Jacob wanted to get a better look at the buddhas, and Ernest stayed with the monkey, who chattered non-stop.

The baskets were surprisingly inexpensive, so the parents bought every one the woman had, thirteen in all. The mother went to get the car while the father and children stayed behind to browse.

"My monkey likes your boy," the shopkeeper gestured at Ernest.

"Where did you get the monkey?" piped in Jacob.

"I found him alone in the alley and we took to one another right away, just like with your brother. What's his name?" asked the shopkeeper.

"Ernest," answered Jacob.

"After Ernest Hemingway," said Abigail.

"And *The Importance of Being Earnest*," added their father.

"He'll have a happier life than either of those Ernests and many more adventures. As will you all," predicted the shopkeeper.

Once the mother returned with the car, the family and the baskets were loaded in. When they edged out of the alley, they all were startled by the brightness of the day and the ordinariness of Kensington Market, which hadn't felt at all ordinary half an hour before.

"Red light up ahead," their father pointed out to their mother as they drove along College Street.

"It's half a block away, Brian," said their mother.

"Just trying to be helpful," said their father. "I'll bet we could never find that place again," he speculated. "It's green now."

"I see the light."

Abigail caught Jacob's eye, and then they both turned to look out of their respective windows.

"At least we have our baskets," said Ernest.

Chapter Two

Apper Dapper Apper Do!

The first laundry adventure happened by accident, which is how these things usually begin. Jacob's hockey practice had been cancelled because of rain, so the family had a little open time on their hands. The parents were in the kitchen making out a grocery list, and Ernest had blasted through the kitchen so many times on his horse Brownie, plastic wheels roaring like a spaceship taking off, that the mother had said, "Brian!" and the father had said, "Everybody upstairs, go get dressed! Right now!" Being ordered to get dressed without help from their parents was something that happened only on the weekends when the children were too noisy or bickered too much. It was a punishment that would sometimes keep the children busy for hours in the era before the thirteen baskets. The parents still used it with the added: "And make your beds too!"

Each person in the family had his own basket, though for some reason all the clothes were still kept in

the parents' bedroom. The rest of the baskets were full of sheets and towels and miscellaneous stuff that no one knew what to do with. Ernest by now had crawled inside one of these miscellaneous baskets and had tied an old apron around his neck like a superhero cape.

"Apper dapper apper do!" Ernest was shouting as he attempted to bury himself under the miscellaneous stuff in the basket.

"Ernest, stop yelling. You're going to make everybody crazy," Jacob said as he peered into the basket. "Hey, do you want me to bury you?"

"Yeah," shouted Ernest. "Apper dapper apper do!"

"Why are you saying that?"

"The monkey told me to. I need to say it, you need to say it. Apper dapper apper do! Jacob, get inside the basket too!"

Jacob clambered into the basket with Ernest, and it felt really good. It was fun jumping around in the laundry, and it was especially fun shouting "Apper dapper apper do!"

Abigail had been in her room painting her fingernails, but the noise was too much for her. As she entered her parents' bedroom she saw Jacob and Ernest jumping up and down in a basket, shouting "Apper dapper apper do!" All of a sudden the basket tipped over and the boys fell quiet. She rushed to see if they were all right, but all she could see were aprons and more aprons spilling out of the basket. Her brothers must be buried deeper inside. She started to crawl into the basket, calling, "Jacob, Ernest!" She could hear her brothers, calling to her from a great distance, saying "Apper dapper apper do!" Suddenly, she felt as if she were falling, and then she tumbled out of the bottom of the basket directly onto Jacob. Jacob let out a bloodcurdling scream and distracted all three of them momentarily from the fact that they were no longer in their parents' bedroom.

They were in a field of soft, wild grass on a prairie. They knew it had to be a prairie because the sky was so big. It looked a lot like Kansas from *The Wizard of Oz*, except for the fact it was in colour, not in black and white.

"We're not in Toronto anymore, Jacob," Ernest said.

"Oh my..." Abigail didn't know what to say.

"Now, I don't think we should be frightened. We've read a lot of books about things like this happening and most of these stories come out pretty well," said Jacob, more trying to convince himself than the others.

"I've read more books than you have, Jacob." Abigail now knew what to say. "I think I should be in charge."

"You're always in charge." Jacob took a deep breath and was about to remind Abigail about the last pirate game that had ended so poorly when Ernest yelled.

"Look."

The children both turned abruptly. Ernest pointed at an old farmhouse with a wraparound porch which sat not thirty feet from where the children had landed. As soon as they saw the farmhouse, they knew it was from another time. They were silent.

A boy of about twelve came out the front door and stood on the porch step. He was wearing a white Stetson hat and looked to be chewing a toothpick. After a minute or so, another younger boy came out. He seemed about eight years old, and he too was wearing a Stetson hat.

"Shore is still," said the younger boy.

"Yup," said the other one.

Abigail and Jacob recognized the accent. They were in Texas.

"Nothin' to see or hear for miles," commented the younger one.

"Nope," said the other one.

The boys were looking directly at our children, who were, in turn, looking at one another.

"We're invisible," announced Ernest.

"Invisible?" said Jacob, slightly choking on the word. "Is that all right?"

"I don't think we have much choice in the matter," Abigail pointed out. "Shh!"

"If they can't see us, they probably can't hear us either," said Ernest.

"No, I want to hear what they're saying," said Abigail.

"We'll bring 'em over to the southeast pasture. I think they're safer from coyotes there," the older boy was saying.

"Coyotes?" gasped Jacob, choking and blanching.

"I know what to do with coyotes," said Ernest.

"No, you don't!" cried Jacob.

"Aline!" called one of the boys on the porch.

"SHH!" hissed Abigail.

"He doesn't know a thing about coyotes," said Jacob.

"Stop it!" ordered Abigail.

"Aline!" called the other boy.

"Just a minute," came a girl's voice from inside the house.

"Mema was Aline," recalled Abigail. "That was her name."

"Mema?" asked Ernest.

"Grandpa's mother," said Abigail. "She died before you were born, Ernest."

"I've seen pictures of her," said Jacob.

"What is it, Garland?" A girl stepped out the front door. She seemed to be between the two boys in age, but the most startling aspect of her appearance was her apron. She was wearing Ernest's superhero apron and Ernest wasn't. The girl gazed out over the prairie, directly at our children.

Our children stared back at her.

"She isn't old," said Ernest.

"We're in the past, Ernest," said Abigail.

"We're time travelling. We're really time travelling!" said Ernest, realizing it for the first time.

"Everything E. Nesbit wrote was true," said Jacob.

"Maybe not everything, Jacob," said Abigail with a slightly superior tone in her voice. Those who knew her would tell you Abigail was a little uneasy with what was going on.

"Ohmygosh, the apple sauce is running over." Aline hurried back into the house.

"Raymond, you go saddle up. Aline, we'll be back by supper," said the older boy.

"Garland..." Aline's voice called from inside.

"Afternoon, sister," said Garland, walking away from the house. "The men have work to do. Father'll have our hides if any more of the herd goes missing." He disappeared into the barn with his brother.

"Let's go with the cowboys, Jacob," suggested Ernest.

"How are we going to do that? We can't run behind the horses, and we can't get on the horses without them knowing it. And we're invisible," said Jacob.

"We'll figure it out. Come on." Ernest grabbed his brother's hand to pull him toward the barn.

"Oh, no!" The children heard a wail from inside the house.

"What's wrong with Mema?" said Abigail.

"I want to fight coyotes. Hurry up, you guys!" cried Ernest.

"They're not going to fight the coyotes, Ernest. They're going to move the cattle," said Jacob.

"Right. Well, let's do that then," proposed Ernest, tugging at Jacob persistently.

Jacob shook himself free. "I don't know about you, but this being invisible makes me a little nervous. Not to mention going into the past. We don't know what's happened or how it works or anything."

"I'm going with the cowboys," announced Ernest.

"You're wearing your pyjamas," said Abigail.

"I'm invisible," said Ernest.

"Maybe not for long. Who knows?" said Jacob.

"What's the point of time travelling if we can't do something fun?" asked Ernest. "They're going to ride away."

Garland and Raymond had led their horses out of the barn, ready to mount and ride off.

Ernest started after them. Abigail grabbed him.

"I want danger and excitement," Ernest declared, trying to pull away from his sister. "I want to see some cows!"

"Stop!" cried Abigail, holding fast to her brother. "We've never even been to the corner store to buy candy without a grown-up. And here we are in the middle Texas a long time in the past—we don't know how long ago—and you want to go fight coyotes and they're not going to fight coyotes and I don't hardly know who those people are and the answer is NO!"

"Grrr," growled Ernest with his fiercest animal growl.

"At least we know Mema," said Abigail, in an effort to calm down.

"Here they come," announced Jacob as Raymond and Garland rode right at them.

Neither the horses nor the cowboys saw the children standing in front of them. Abigail, Jacob and Ernest jumped aside.

"I sure wish sister would learn to cook," Raymond was saying.

"Yup," agreed Garland.

Just as Garland's horse passed by, Ernest lunged for a stirrup, but Abigail held him back. The cowboys rode off in silence.

"Grrr," repeated Ernest.

"Stop it," said Abigail.

"The most exciting event in my life turns out to be the most boring. I want to go with the cowboys," Ernest insisted.

"Maybe we can have a different kind of adventure," suggested Abigail, without being sure.

"A sissy adventure," sighed Ernest.

"I can't believe that the first time we leave the house without Mommy and Daddy, we leave in our pyjamas," moaned Abigail.

"At least nobody can see us," said Jacob, realizing the advantage of invisibility.

"Shhh!" shushed Abigail. "Listen."

"I don't hear anything," said Jacob. "It's quieter

even than Muskoka."

"Imagine, coming on an adventure and discovering quiet," said Ernest, unhappily. But Ernest began to concentrate upon the silence: he couldn't help it.

The Toronto children had never heard quiet that deep or long, from horizon to horizon. It felt uncomfortable at first, to be in the midst of all that silence, and then it started to feel marvellous and free, like swimming in a lake when the water is no longer cold. Abigail, Jacob and Ernest just had to lie down in the wispy prairie grass and watch the clouds, flat-bottomed and puffy on the top, languidly float by. They didn't think about the clouds or the stillness or where they were; they didn't think at all. It was divine.

And then, on the wind, as if it was an act of the imagination, a note was heard, followed by another and another and another, until it was clear that there was music somewhere, somewhere in the distance.

The children lay in the grass and listened. The tunes were unfamiliar, and the haunting, airy sound was unlike any sound they'd ever heard before.

They heard the screen door gently close, followed by the briefest sound of footsteps, then nothing but the music.

When Ernest sat up, he saw the girl, Aline, his great-grandmother, walk across the grassy field and stop. She stood still to listen to the music on the breeze.

Silently, all three rose and started walking toward Aline. She held her head tilted up against the breeze, her eyes closed to let the air and the music wash over her. When she opened her eyes, Abigail felt she could see a deep longing in Aline's face, a yearning for sounds beyond the horizon. Then the moment ended.

Aline turned her head and caught sight of figures approaching her. She let out a cry.

Abigail, Jacob and Ernest stopped moving and let out cries (or rather gasps) of their own; they hadn't expected to be seen.

Abigail was closest to Aline, and the girls couldn't help but stare at one another. They were about the same age and the same height, with the same clear and lively eyes, though Aline's were velvet brown.

"Mother's gonna kill me for comin' out without a bonnet," said Aline, starting to fidget with her apron. The apron was a gooey mess of applesauce and what looked like soapsuds.

"Who are you?" she asked.

No one knew what to say. There was a silence. Finally Abigail spoke: "My brothers and I are travelling."

"Y'all are not from around here?" asked Aline, noticing the difference in accent right away.

"No," said Jacob.

"Golly, for a second I thought y'all were

escaped convicts in those uniforms," said Aline, in a most kindhearted way.

"Our blue cozies," said Ernest, referring to the blue flannel pyjamas their mother had made them last Christmas.

"We left this morning in a hurry," explained Jacob.

"Goodness," said Aline.

"It's so embarrassing," said Abigail.

"Don't you worry 'bout your gear. I sure don't mind. I'm Aline."

"I'm Ernest, and this is Jacob and Abigail," said Ernest.

There was another silence, disturbed only by the barely audible music. The four children listened for a moment.

"What kind of music is that?" asked Jacob.

"Isn't it beautiful? It's from a Victrola over at the Currie place, 'bout a mile from here," said Aline.

"A Victrola?" said Ernest, who didn't recognize the word.

"You wind it up and it plays music, but music somebody else played in the past. The music isn't alive. I'm not very good at explaining."

"The music is recorded," said Jacob.

"That's right. Some people call it a

phonograph. It's brand new. I heard it first last week when my brothers and I went over. Now they play it almost every day. I love it," said Aline.

"Maybe you could ask your parents to buy you one," suggested Ernest.

"No, we need our money for other things. Mother an' Father have gone to see a man about some cattle feed," said Aline.

"And they left you here alone?" asked Abigail, unable to hide her shock.

"They'll only be gone a couple days. Golly, Mother'll kill me if I freckle up. I've got to go inside," announced Aline.

"Freckle up?" asked Jacob.

"You know, ruin my complexion. I'll never find a husband then."

Abigail remembered that her mother told her Mema (Aline) had married at sixteen. The couple had eloped to the next county and married secretly. Aline didn't tell her parents about the wedding until a few days later.

"Oh, I'm sure you'll find a husband," said Abigail, feeling a little strange that a girl her own age would even be thinking about such things. But Aline was her great-grandmother, and it was a different time.

"I worry about it," said Aline as she started towards the house.

Ernest slipped his hand into hers. Jacob would have

taken her other hand, but the mess of applesauce and soapsuds on her apron looked really sickening.

"Y'all hungry?" asked Aline.

Jacob was definitely not, but Ernest answered, "We're always hungry!"

"Well, I can look after y'all," said Aline. "Not to insult you in the least, but y'all look as if you could do with a little lookin' after."

Abigail, Jacob and Ernest accepted the "lookin' after" as entirely normal. After all, she was their great-grandmother, even if she was only ten years old.

The four children entered the house. It was small and sparsely furnished. The kitchen ran from front to back along one side. On the other side were three curtained doors, leading to what must be three tiny bedrooms. At the front end of the kitchen were a rocker and a couple of more or less comfortable chairs. Hanging from the ceiling was a large wooden frame with a half-finished patchwork quilt. At the back end of the kitchen were a table and five straight-backed chairs, a kerosene stove, a water pump and a rough-looking china cabinet full of dishes.

What caught the children's attention most, however, were the dirty dishes and bits of old food cluttered beside the water pump and a broom and unemptied dustbin in the middle of the floor. The stove looked like a volcano had just erupted, with a saucepan burnt black and applesauce dripping down the sides of the stove like lava. A bowl with soapy water sat on the floor beside the stove.

"Goodness," said Aline, "it is a mess."

"This is what you were yelling about when your brothers were leaving," said Abigail.

"They have their jobs and I have mine," sighed Aline.

"We all should have gone with them," said Ernest.

"Ernest!" said Abigail as she slapped her brother on the shoulder for being so insensitive.

"I don't want to go with them," said Aline. "I don't care one bit about horses and cattle, except as how we make our living. I don't want to be a boy, but I'm not very good at being a girl."

"What do you mean 'being a girl'?" asked Jacob.

"Cooking and cleaning and remembering your bonnet, I don't do any of those things well," explained Aline, picking up the broom and dustbin.

"Abigail is a girl, and she doesn't do any of those things," said Ernest.

"You don't either," said Abigail. "I mean, we're children. Our parents would never leave us to look after ourselves."

"Well, on our farm everybody has to help in the ways that they're supposed to. I'm the only girl. I've got to do the girl work." Aline sighed again.

"In our house we don't have boy work or girl work," said Jacob, collecting the dirty dishes. Both Ernest and Abigail joined in with the tidy-up.

"You're lucky," said Aline, slumping into one of the kitchen chairs. She seemed to drift off a little. Her three great-grandchildren busied themselves cleaning the kitchen.

As Ernest scraped plates and started washing dishes (he'd never washed a dish in his life), he imagined the cowboys and horses and cattle, and he started feeling let down. This adventure was deeply disappointing.

Abigail felt confused by the situation. It was stupid that girls had to do certain things just because they were girls, but then Aline wasn't doing anything, and they were doing all her work. She wasn't looking after them at all. Abigail did not like the direction this adventure was taking either.

As for Jacob, he couldn't really think of anything but controlling his urge to throw up. He was scraping that gross mess of applesauce off the stove. He didn't really know why he was doing it, but he was doing it, and in order to control his heaving stomach, he had to make his mind go blank.

Our children worked until the clean-up was nearly finished and Aline sat at the table with the longing expression Abigail had noticed outside, as if she were yearning for the distance. Then suddenly, she announced: "It's called 'Little Star'."

Startled, Abigail, Jacob and Ernest turned from their tasks.

"My poem," explained Aline, "the one I just came up with." She began to recite.

A baby star was
shining
Along the Milky Way.
She said I'm tired
of twinkling. I wish
it would be day.

Her Mama gently
tucked her in.
She knew it would
be best.
For little baby stars
do need
a lot of time to rest.

"Did you just make that up?" asked Jacob.

"Yes, I must have been thinking about y'all in your pyjamas," explained Aline.

"It didn't look like you were doing anything. We were doing all the work," said Ernest.

"We were doing the work that you can see. There are other kinds of work," Abigail realized all of a sudden.

"I've never told anybody one of my poems before, but I want y'all to know them," said Aline, tenderly.

"Abigail makes up poems," announced Ernest.

"Ernest!"

"You don't have to be embarrassed, Abigail. I'm not," said Aline. "I'd like to hear one of your poems."

"Oh, all right," agreed Abigail. Everyone sat down at the table, and Abigail recited her poem.

A Card Game in the Dark

My family
Sits around a barrel
Cut in half
Upside down
Cards thrown all over
My brother makes me pick up two
With a silly grin on his face
My four-year-old brother
Beats us again!
Nobody else
Ever wins.

Night closes in around us
The porch light
Is burning out
The dog whining
In the background
My brother
In a T-shirt and underwear
Oh my gosh!
He's won again!

"The poem is a true story," said Ernest. "About me."

"I might have guessed that," said Aline. "I like it. It has a real feeling."

"Thanks. I have others," said Abigail.

"So do I," said Aline.

And so the children sat at the table through the afternoon, exchanging poems and talking. Aline brought out some soda crackers and butter and sugar and the children made themselves a snack. The afternoon passed quickly, though at one point Ernest imagined himself riding with real cowboys, herding cattle instead of sitting at a kitchen table. This adventure confused him: he liked it well enough, but it wasn't what he really wanted. He wanted motion and excitement.

All of a sudden, a voice came from outside the house. "Sister, you got two boys out here hungry as jackrabbits. We'll get the horses fed and watered and be in for supper."

"Oh, no!" cried Aline, "I haven't done anything."

"We should go," said Abigail, who suddenly remembered her parents back in Toronto.

"Won't y'all stay and visit with my brothers?" said Aline, bustling about to set the table.

"No, thank you," said Abigail.

"We can be your secret friends," suggested Ernest.

"Well, y'all are the only ones who know my poems," said Aline. "I guess that does make us secret friends. Y'all sure about your way back home?"

"I think so," said Jacob. "Right, Ernest?"

"I can't remember everything the monkey told me, but..."

"Ernest!" interrupted Jacob.

"If y'all get lost, you come right back here. I don't want you wandering around at night with coyotes on the loose," warned Aline.

"I forgot about the coyotes," said Ernest, excitedly.

Abigail, Jacob and Ernest stepped out the front door just as Garland and Raymond were coming out of the barn. As before, our children were invisible to Aline's brothers.

"They'll never love us the way Mema does," said Ernest.

"Is that why Aline sees us and they don't?" asked Jacob.

Ernest shrugged.

"OK, Ernest, what do we do now?" asked Abigail. "You got us here. Get us home."

"It's easy. We just jump up and down and shout 'Apper dapper apper do'!" said Ernest.

So the three children tramped out into the field, close to where they'd arrived, and they yelled and they jumped and they yelled and they jumped and they yelled "Apper dapper apper do!" ever more loudly, but nothing happened.

"Oh no!" moaned Jacob. The pleasures of the afternoon evaporated. The silence and the music and the poems lost their charms. The calm they'd felt turned into panic.

"We're trapped here. We'll never see Mommy and Daddy again," wailed Abigail.

"We'll have to start eating meat because we're in Texas," said Jacob. (Our children were vegetarians.)

"Huh?" said Ernest.

"We're more likely to be eaten by the coyotes," said Abigail.

"What are we going to do?" asked Jacob.

"I can't remember," said Ernest miserably.

"Ernest!" said Abigail, her teeth locked shut.

"Something must be different," said Ernest.

"The apron. You're not wearing the apron," said Jacob, recovering himself.

"She's wearing it!" grimaced Abigail in despair.

"If we go back in there, she'll see us and they won't, and they'll think she's crazy, and that won't be nice at all," figured Jacob.

"She believes in us, they don't," said Ernest.

"Let's go around back and see if we can get her attention," said Abigail.

"I don't want to get her into any trouble," said Jacob. "Especially since she doesn't have her brothers' dinner ready."

Abigail gave Jacob a very cold look.

As they walked around the house, our children could hear Raymond and Garland talking to Aline.

"Let's just eat the cold chicken," said one boy.

"I'll sure be glad when Mother's back," said the other.

A big splash was heard and then Aline's voice: "Not again!"

Just as the children reached the back, Aline rushed out the back door, untying her soaking apron. She wrung it out and pegged it on a clothesline to dry. She was preoccupied and didn't see her visitors.

When the door slammed behind Aline, Abigail took the apron off the line and tied it, still wet and gooey, around Ernest's neck. Jacob tried not to look at the apron.

The children hurried away from the house. Just before they started to jump up and down again, Abigail asked her brothers, "Do you think they've noticed that we're gone?"

"Who?" asked Ernest.

"Our parents!" said Abigail and Jacob.

As it happened, the parents did notice the quiet of the house and figured their children were deep in a game. Like most parents, these two loved nothing more than knowing their children were, if briefly, content with one another in companionable imaginary lands. Chaos was held at bay.

"I'd better start the laundry," the father finally announced. He started up the stairs as the mother tidied up the breakfast dishes.

Chapter Three

Daddy

Over eighty years and thousands of miles passed in a flash. The children didn't realize they were home until they heard their father's voice boom down at them: "Out of the laundry, you three. You're going to break these baskets, and then where would we be?"

The children could have said "in Texas," but they didn't. They didn't say anything.

The father found it a bit peculiar his children didn't rise to the bait of an argument, but the change was refreshing, and he decided not to comment on it.

"Is supper ready?" asked Ernest.

"Supper? You just had breakfast," replied the father.

"What time is it, Daddy?" asked Jacob.

"It's about ten-thirty," answered the father.

"Ten-thirty!" the three responded altogether. They had spent hours with Aline, but time hadn't passed at all in Toronto.

"That's very interesting," said Jacob as he and Abigail

looked at each other, realizing that time travel worked in life as it often did in books: present time stopped while children traipsed through the past (or the future).

"What have you kids been up to?" asked the father.

"Oh, you know, playing a game," said Abigail, trying to sound casual.

"Well, it's time to get dressed. And stay out of the laundry!" The father picked up the basket full of dirty clothes and started awkwardly down the hall to the stairs.

The basket was large and very heavy, and the children noticed a certain radiance to the wicker they hadn't noticed before. It was as if there was a soft light shining inside the basket. The other twelve baskets in the bedroom had started to glow with that same soft light.

"What do you think that means?" asked Abigail.

"I don't know," replied Jacob.

"It's magic!" announced Ernest.

"Laundry magic," said Abigail. "It's nothing like the books, though."

"I liked being with Mema," said Jacob.

"So did I. But it was different from wrestling coyotes," said Ernest.

"Wrestling coyotes!" Abigail and Jacob said together as they rolled their eyes.

"E. Nesbit always had someone to explain the magic,

the Phoenix or the Psammead," said Abigail.

"This is life," reminded Jacob.

"The monkey explained it all to me," said Ernest.

"But you forget things," said Jacob.

"You get confused," said Abigail.

"I love laundry!" shouted Ernest, dumping out one of the baskets.

"Not so loud!" snapped Abigail.

"I love adventures, even apron adventures!" said Ernest, not shouting but doing a version of the backstroke through the laundry he'd dumped.

"Don't be so annoying. And you're making a big mess. I'm not cleaning it up." Jacob hated tidying up after Ernest.

"Why did Mema see us when the others didn't?" wondered Abigail, settling into the rocking chair.

"She has to believe in us," suggested Jacob, who was perched on the edge of the bed. "We're her descendants."

Ernest, who'd stopped doing the backstroke and looked now as if he were simply floating on the sea of laundry, added: "Believers in the future."

"The weird thing is she didn't see us at first. She had to be alone to notice us," said Jacob.

"What does it all mean?" asked Abigail.

"I don't know," said Jacob. "I got the feeling she really cared about us even though she didn't know we're related. She had no idea who we were."

"That's true," agreed Abigail.

They looked over to Ernest, who had fallen asleep on the laundry pile.

"I want to have another adventure," said Jacob.

"So do I," said Abigail. "It's funny. I guess we don't have to go to Ancient Egypt or Atlantis for our adventures. To be free."

"I guess," agreed Jacob. "It's weird following *him*, though," gesturing to Ernest, "isn't it?"

"You can say that again," agreed Abigail.

Ernest snorted in his sleep and rolled over. Abigail covered him up with a towel from another laundry basket. "He looks almost sweet when he's asleep."

Jacob didn't answer. He'd retreated up to his bedroom to rearrange his hockey cards and to think about his secrets. Later Abigail redid her nails, blue and yellow polka dots this time, and thought about her secrets. Ernest had a good long nap. He revealed his dreams to no one.

✳ ✳ ✳

Through the following week, the children were unusually quiet. They didn't wrestle or argue or shriek at each other; they were kind and considerate. Readers and writers of storybook magic would have declared Abigail, Jacob and Ernest good enough to have earned more magic.

Their father was a writer for the Corporation, and he had to work this Saturday afternoon. The children decided it would be a good day for another adventure; they just had to get their mother out of the way first. Even if time didn't work the same when they were in the past, they didn't want any awkward surprises.

"Mommy?"

"Yes. Abigail."

Her mother was sitting at the kitchen table tapping away at a portable typewriter. She didn't look up from her work.

"Mommy?"

"There we go, 'Indignantly yours'. Now I just have to find an envelope."

"Who are you writing to?"

"The government. I certainly hope they pay attention this time. It's like writing into a void, a black hole in time and space."

"Oh," said Abigail before she changed the subject. "It's been a long time since you made a lemon meringue pie."

"Has it?"

"Months, I think. We sure love those pies."

"I know you do, and you and your brothers are such good children." Abigail's mother started to get a bit teary. "Why don't I make a pie this afternoon?"

"That would be wonderful, Mommy."

"The only problem is that it takes so long. Do you think you could keep your brothers busy while I bake?"

"I already have a game in mind," said Abigail.

"You're such a sweet girl," said her mother, tears by this time rolling down her face. "You know I love you."

"I love you too. Bye." Abigail skipped out of the kitchen and up the stairs to the laundry baskets, where her brothers were waiting. "It was easy," she told them. "She's crying now, but she's going to make a pie."

"I better go and cheer her up," said Jacob, who tended to worry when people were sad.

"Don't bother. It's just her 'I love you kids' cry. She'll get over it. We'd better get going."

The children had spent the week secretly debating where to go on their next adventure. They figured that Ernest had to wear the piece of laundry that would connect them to another time and place—after all, that's how it had worked last time. They rifled through the laundry, trying to imagine where this sock or that undershirt might take them.

Abigail finally settled on the idea of unpacking the baby museum (a trunk full of clothes and mementos from when they were younger) and going back into their own histories. Of course, Abigail wanted to go back to her babyhood, Jacob to his and Ernest didn't really care as long as he had some kind of adventure.

While the other two argued, Ernest foraged through the baby museum on his own and pulled out a baby sweater. He tied the sleeves under his chin and wore it like a bonnet. He then climbed into a laundry basket and started to jump up and down.

"Apper dapper apper do! Apper dapper apper do!" Ernest began to chant.

"Oh no! He's going without us!" Abigail and Jacob realized.

"Hurry up, Jacob!" Abigail ordered. She pushed him into the basket. "Wait for me!"

"Apper dapper apper do!" Jacob joined in.

"Apper dapper apper do!" chimed in Abigail.

Silence.

"You kids all right up there?" The children's mother had heard the racket. "Abigail, Jacob, Ernest?"

"We're fine." Abigail's voice sounded as if it were coming from inside a tunnel far, far away.

"Well, let me know if you need anything," said their mother as she returned to piecing together her piecrust.

"Okaaaa..."

It was a gentler landing for the children this time. First of all, they knew more of what to expect and didn't fight the fall and, this time, instead of landing on the hard prairie, they landed on a sand dune, steps away from an ocean. There was no one in sight, though a huge bonfire burned on the beach.

The children were thrilled to be at a seashore, even if they didn't know which sea it was.

"I'm going in the water," Abigail announced as she tugged at her clothes.

"I want to ride a wave," Ernest shouted as he hurriedly pulled off his sweater.

"You'd better leave your underwear on, you don't know who's going to show up," Jacob advised. Jacob rarely took all his clothes off. In fact, in the summer, he always wore his socks (albeit unmatched socks) in the back yard. Being at the ocean inspired him though, and he started to undress.

"Don't worry," said Abigail, "we're probably invisible anyway. I plan to skinny dip for my first swim in the ocean."

"Skinny dipping! Hurrah!" applauded Ernest.

"What are we going to do with our clothes?" asked Jacob.

"Oh, just leave them on the beach," said Abigail, "They're as invisible as we are. I can't wait to get in that water."

Abigail ran ahead of the others and jumped into the

ocean. "Hah! Hah! It's cold!" She bounced over the waves for a minute or so, and then plugged her nose and dunked herself. When she surfaced she looked just like a mermaid.

Jacob and Ernest were slower into the water and just as shocked by the temperature, but very soon all three were leaping into the waves and riding the currents until their tummies got scratched in the sand. Everything they'd ever read or heard about the ocean was true. They loved the saltiness on their skin and the buoyancy and the roughness of the waves. They loved the feel of sand as it moved under their feet and they loved the feeling of coming up from under a wave and not knowing where they were. They played and played and played and were very happy until Jacob looked down the beach and realized they had gradually moved far from the bonfire and the spot where they'd left their clothes.

"Come on," he said, "we've got to get back."

"It's okay as long as we can see the bonfire," said Abigail.

As the children continued to play and jump and dive and float and take complete pleasure in their adventure and their lives, they forgot that the ocean has tides. When they looked up sometime later, the bonfire appeared closer to the water. This was when they decided they really had better get back to the bonfire.

The children realized almost at once that their

clothes were no longer on the beach.

"We'll just go home," announced Abigail.

"I don't know if it'll work," said Ernest. "We don't have any laundry."

Jacob, who was very thin, started to shiver.

"Let's try," insisted Abigail.

"Apper dapper apper do, apper dapper apper do," chanted the children, trying for enthusiasm.

"It's not going to work," said Ernest.

"Not if we don't jump up and down. Come on, you guys!" said Abigail.

"Apper dapper apper do. Apper dapper apper do." The children jumped up and down, but nothing happened.

"We're spirits now. We're not connected to anything," said Ernest.

"That's insane!" Abigail was impatient.

Jacob's teeth were chattering even louder. He was starting to turn blue.

"Jacob! Let's go over to the fire. Come on, Ernest. I don't want you talking nonsense now."

"It isn't nonsense, Abigail, it's true. We're going to miss that lemon meringue pie. I miss Mommy!" Ernest started to cry.

Abigail hustled her brothers over to the bonfire and settled them on a log, close to the fire. She rubbed Jacob's shoulders, and she wiped away Ernest's tears. She then settled herself between the boys and they all huddled together. They were all too afraid to speak.

After all, they didn't even know where they were.

Some time later, no one knew how long, they heard a voice approaching.

"That's a darlin' now. I want you to stay here by the fire while I run and pick up a couple of things for supper."

The voice was vaguely familiar to the children, but they couldn't place it. Nor could they place the thin, nervous-looking woman attached to it. She had pushed an old-fashioned baby carriage along a path they hadn't seen before. The carriage was decorated with tissue paper and was far enough back from the fire that they couldn't see who or what was inside.

"Have a nice long sleep now, darlin'," said the woman as she turned and disappeared over a hill.

"At least they speak English here," said Jacob.

"Let's see what's in that carriage. Why do you think it's all dolled up like that?" Abigail wondered.

"It's the pot of gold at the end of the rainbow!" Ernest shouted, as he ran over to the carriage. He drew a hat covered in gold coins out of the carriage. "See!"

"Maybe they're chocolate," said Jacob, as he and Abigail joined Ernest.

"Shhh!" said Abigail, as she noticed a baby sleeping in the carriage. The baby was big, at least a year old or maybe older, and it had an angelic face. It was nestled into the carriage with a number of blankets. Abigail gently lifted one of the blankets out and handed it to

Jacob. She had taken another out and was wrapping Ernest up when the baby started to cry. Abigail quickly grabbed the last blanket for herself and was struggling to tie it up like a sarong when Jacob asked: "Is this baby going to see us?"

"All babies see things other people don't," answered Ernest.

"How do you know all this stuff, Ernest?" asked Jacob. He turned to Abigail, "I think he makes it all up."

The baby was really starting to howl when it rolled over and lifted itself up to look over the edge of the carriage. As soon as it saw the children, and it definitely saw them, it started to laugh and smile at them and say "Hi! Hi! Hi!" in a sweet little baby voice.

"It does see us," said Jacob, shocked at the fact.

"It isn't an 'it', he's a 'he'," said Abigail, "Look at the cowboys on his pants. Nobody dresses a girl that way."

The three children gathered closer to the carriage. They gasped.

"Oh, my goodness!" said Abigail.

The baby was wearing the sweater Ernest had had on his head at the beginning of this adventure. He reached out to Abigail for her to pick him up.

"He definitely likes us," said Jacob.

The baby was very heavy, so Abigail set him down on the beach. The children sat around him and he reached out to each of them, grasping hands and kissing them, stroking Abigail, Jacob and Ernest's

cheeks and saying "Hi! Hi! Hi!" and smiling and laughing all the time.

"He doesn't just like us, he *really* likes us," said Jacob.

"There's something so familiar about him," said Abigail. "I feel that when I look into his eyes I see..."

"Daddy?" asked Ernest.

"Yeah," said Abigail.

"It's weird. You *can* see Daddy inside this baby," said Jacob.

"Brian? Are you Brian?" Abigail asked the baby and he clapped his hands. "Are we in Nova Scotia, I wonder?"

"Does he know we're his children?" asked Jacob.

"How could he know that, he's a baby. He knows he likes us, and that's all that's important," said Abigail.

"He loves pie. Remember how happy Daddy is when he has pie? " said Ernest.

"What's that got to do with anything?" asked Jacob. "Do we call him Daddy or Brian?"

"I think we should call him 'Brian'. The Daddy part would only confuse him now," said Abigail.

"Brian loves pie," said Ernest.

"You know, I'm really hungry," said Jacob.

"Brian and I are too," said Ernest.

Abigail stood up. She looked serious. "It's possible, now that we've got the sweater here, we could zip home, get on some warm clothes, have a snack... "

"Pie!" interrupted Ernest.

"Right, and return Brian before Nana comes back to pick him up."

"You mean take Daddy with us?" Jacob asked.

"Brian," corrected Abigail.

The baby started to clap his hands again.

"What would we tell Mommy?"

"Jacob, we're not going to be home long enough for Mommy to find out anything. I'm hungry and wet and cold, and I want to go home. I don't want to leave Brian here. He'd be too sad if we went without him, and he'll certainly howl," Abigail's voice was shaking.

"What if Nana comes back and he's not here?" Jacob asked.

"We need the sweater to get back and it hardly seems fair to take that off and just leave him, cold and lonely," said Abigail. "And look how cute he is!"

"A missing baby is a missing baby, Abigail. It's kidnapping. Nana will be very upset," said Jacob.

"Then we just have to move quickly," announced Abigail. "I'm going home. Ernest, let's go."

While Abigail and Jacob had been talking, Ernest had buried himself and Brian in sand. The older children had to brush the two younger ones off, and they all held hands while jumping up and down shouting "Apper dapper apper do! Apper dapper apper do!"

Moments before the four children were raced back to the present time, Ernest hollered triumphantly above the crashing of the waves: "I'm not the youngest anymore!"

Chapter Four

Stardust

It was a very tight fit in the laundry basket when the children arrived home again. The baskets were barely large enough for three children, and four made it painful. Babies are bigger than one first imagines.

The children heard an earthy moan from the basket as they spilled out onto the floor of their parents' bedroom. "Uuuuuhhhh," was the sound, and it made the hair on the back of their necks stand up.

"Do you think we wrecked the basket?" Abigail asked.

Jacob gave the basket a once over and reported: "It looks okay to me. It's starting to glow with that kind of radiating light like last time, but that's probably normal."

All of the baskets began to glow just enough to notice.

"They're celebrating," explained Ernest.

Abigail and Jacob just looked at their brother. They didn't want to know.

The important thing was to get dressed as quickly as possible, keep the Baby Brian hidden from their

mother and have a snack—preferably lemon meringue pie—before they rushed back to Nova Scotia, 1951.

While Abigail, Jacob and Ernest were rooting around the laundry, searching for something to wear, Baby Brian sifted through part of the laundry himself. Every time he found a shirt or a sock or a pair of pants belonging to the grown-up Brian, Baby Brian would coo or sigh or giggle and hold the article close to himself. The others didn't pay too much attention to his behaviour, but when Baby Brian found a corduroy dress belonging to their mother he let out a big sigh, held the dress to his chest and stuck his finger in his mouth.

"Isn't that Mommy's going-out-to-dinner dress?" asked Jacob.

"Yeah," answered Abigail, "but she hasn't worn it for a year or so."

"They should go out more often," said Jacob as he gestured to Baby Brian, who was stroking the dress affectionately.

When the phone rang beside her, Abigail picked it up. It was her father wanting to talk with her mother. Abigail stayed on to listen when her mother picked up the downstairs line.

"I'm going to come home right away," he said.

"Are you all right?" she asked.

"No. I feel very strange, and it happened all of a sudden," he said.

"What happened? Are you sick?"

"I feel like I'm fading away. I've never felt this way before, and it's frightening." His voice seemed faint.

"Brian!" She sounded alarmed. "I'll come and get you."

"No, you'd have to pack up all the kids and come downtown. I'm going to take a taxi. I forgot my keys today, and I wanted to make sure you're home."

"I'm not going anywhere. I'm making a pie. Your favourite."

"I don't feel much like eating. Bye." He hung up.

Abigail turned to her brothers, "We've got to take Baby Brian back right away."

"I don't understand," said Jacob.

"I don't either. But his being here is making Daddy

sick somehow and I'm scared," said Abigail.

"Daddy sick?" Jacob couldn't stand the thought of anyone in pain or unwell. He froze.

"Ernest, hurry up and get some socks on. We have to go back immediately." Abigail used her older sister voice.

"I don't want to take the baby back. I love him and besides, he's the littlest now." Ernest was sitting beside Brian, playing peekaboo with his mother's dress.

"We can't argue about this, Ernest. It just has to happen."

Jacob returned to himself. "Abigail, maybe we can take him back without Ernest. It's crowded in that basket."

"I'm not going anywhere without Ernest. However weird it is, he's the only one who understands what's going on a lot of the time," said Abigail.

"I wouldn't say he's on top of the situation right now," offered Jacob.

But Jacob was wrong. Only Ernest had heard footsteps on the stairs, and he managed to toss a bathrobe over Brian just as their mother entered the room.

"How many times have I asked you guys not to play in my bedroom?" Their mother looked very upset. "Daddy's coming home from work early because he isn't feeling well, and I want this room tidy so he can rest. Why is this room such a mess?"

The children didn't have time to answer, even if they did have an answer, because their mother noticed right away that they'd changed their clothes.

"What happened to the clothes you were all wearing earlier? No, don't answer. I don't want to know. What am I going to do?" Their mother slumped down beside the bed and put her head in her hands.

For a moment the children just watched their mother; she hadn't had a laundry meltdown since they'd bought the baskets. They were expecting all the usual questions: "Why am I the only one who ever puts anything away? Why can't you put your dirty clothes in the dirty clothes pile? What am I going to do?" when Baby Brian did a very Brian-like thing. He climbed out from under the bathrobe, stood up and dumped it into a basket. The children gasped. Their mother was startled out of her reverie. Their father was not a great organizer, but he always liked things tidy. So, it appeared, did the baby. Their mother was too shocked at first to say anything. A strange baby was doing what she had moments ago resigned herself yet again to doing—picking up the laundry.

Suddenly Ernest righted a basket that had toppled over and started to fill it with laundry. Abigail and Jacob joined in, and the four children worked diligently until all trace of laundry disappeared. Baby Brian then crawled onto the mother's lap and gave her a big wet kiss on the cheek.

"Kids?" Their mother still appeared to be in shock.

"I've always wanted a baby brother," announced Ernest.

"Ernest, we can't keep him." Jacob was annoyed.

"We have to take him back right away, don't we, Mommy?" Abigail was trying to remain calm.

"Back where? Where did you get this baby?"

Lady, the dog, started to bark downstairs.

"There's your father home from work. We can't let him see the baby now, he's too ill. The last thing he needs is a surprise. Take the baby up to the playroom and I'll get your father settled. I want to know what's going on."

As the children went up the stairs, their mother called out: "Keep quiet up there now!"

The playroom was just above their parents' bedroom and similarly shaped; instead of laundry spread all over, there were toys.

The four children could hear muffled voices from below. Eventually the door was pulled shut and they heard their mother coming up the stairs.

"What are we going to tell her?" Jacob was very anxious.

"I don't know," answered Abigail.

"Let's tell her the truth," suggested Ernest.

"Don't be stupid!" Abigail and Jacob said together.

"I want a baby brother!" Ernest started to cry.

"He can't be your brother, he's your father," whispered Abigail between her teeth.

The baby picked up a toy fire truck and gave it to Ernest.

Their mother entered the playroom, swept part of the futon clear of toys and sat down. "Who is this baby?" she asked.

No one answered.

The baby climbed onto her lap again, and their mother seemed to relax a little. Her face looked less stern. "He's very sweet," she said. "It's funny, there's something so familiar about him."

Suddenly there was a blood-curdling scream from downstairs, "Arraaaagh!"

"It's your father. Everybody stay here!" Their mother put Baby Brian down on the floor and ran downstairs.

"What's going on?" asked Jacob, looking very rattled.

"I don't know exactly," said Abigail, "But I'm pretty sure it has something to do with Baby Brian being here. It's not healthy for Daddy to have himself as a baby in the same time and place or something. We have to get him back to Nana right away."

All of a sudden there was another blood-curdling scream from downstairs, this time from their mother: "Arraaaagh!"

Abigail picked up Baby Brian, and the four children rushed down to their parents' bedroom. They left the baby outside the door and crowded in.

Their mother was sprawled out on the floor, unconscious. As Abigail caught sight of her, the thought went through her head that the one time her mother could have used laundry spread all over the floor, it was tidied up. She tried to rouse her mother, patting her cheeks hard (as she'd seen in the movies), but her mother didn't respond.

Jacob and Ernest were transfixed by their father on the bed. He was passing one of his hands through the other; he performed this action repeatedly, as if he weren't completely made of matter anymore. It was like he was made of stardust, with only the outline of a human being. He didn't seem to notice anyone else in the room.

With the children distracted, Baby Brian crawled into the room and lifted himself up the side of the bed. The closer he got to grown-up Brian, the more stardusty and less human grown-up Brian became.

Jacob grabbed the baby and caught Ernest's arm. He

dragged them both over to a laundry basket and he ordered Ernest in, then he put the baby in. He crawled in himself and called to Abigail, "Hurry up!"

Abigail tried to lower herself in, but it was crowded. Without any discussion, the children all started to chant "Apper dapper apper do! Apper dapper apper do!" They jumped up and down the best they could in that confined space and then they were gone.

As they whooshed back in time, a tiny voice pleaded, "Snack?"

Chapter Five

Yesterday a Bachelor, Today a Grandpa

If Brian wanted a snack, they had all landed in the right place, though none of the children knew that at first. The experience of landing was highly unpleasant; they found themselves on a hard floor under a table, complete with tablecloth, surrounded by hundreds of pairs of feet they could see milling around them.

"Where are we?" whispered Jacob.

"Ernest, what were you hanging on to in the laundry basket?" asked Abigail, also whispering.

"I don't know," said Ernest, not whispering.

"Shh!" said Jacob and Abigail.

"Shh!" imitated Brian.

"Oh no," said Abigail under her breath, "he's starting to act like a brother."

"We must be at a wedding," said Jacob.

The children turned their attention to the lower portion of an ivory satin wedding gown standing beside the legs of a crisply pressed blue suit. "I wonder who's getting married," said Abigail.

"We'll never know from this angle," Jacob pointed out. "I'd think we're pretty much guaranteed invisibility in this crowd. What do you think, Ernest?"

"Let's eat," said Ernest.

When the children crawled out from under the table, they found themselves faced with an image they'd seen hundreds of times on the wall of their grandmother's study.

"They're just like in the picture," blurted Jacob, more than a little startled.

The bride and groom were standing in front of a three-tiered wedding cake, offering one another a piece.

"It's amazing," said Abigail.

"Yeah," agreed Ernest. "Who are they?"

"Grandma and Grandpa!" snapped Abigail. "Come on!"

"They sure don't look like Grandma and Grandpa," said Ernest. "Grandpa has a moustache."

"Not when he was young," said Jacob.

"Grandma's hair is a different colour."

"Ernest," said Jacob impatiently, "they're young."

"Oh," said Ernest.

"I wonder if they'll see us," said Abigail.

"There's so many people here. Do you know where we are?" asked Jacob.

"The basement of the First Methodist Church, Jamestown, New York," announced Abigail, surprising even herself that she had that information. "It's September 27th, 1952."

"Wow!" said Ernest.

"Yeah, wow!" said Jacob. "We're sure off course."

"Hey, where's Brian?" asked Abigail.

The children suddenly realized their father had crawled away somewhere. A hasty survey of the room didn't produce him, but the room was packed, and he could be anywhere.

"You go that way," Abigail gestured to Jacob, "and I'll go that way and Ernest, you stay here."

Abigail and Jacob scoured the room and couldn't find a trace of Brian. When they returned to the table with the wedding cake, Ernest too had disappeared.

"Do you think they went back without us?" asked Jacob.

"Ernest wouldn't do that. There's got to be a perfectly logical explanation," said Abigail.

"We're not living in a logical world, Abigail. Surely time travel has reminded you of that."

"That may be true, but people do what's logical to them. What would Brian do at a wedding reception?"

"Daddy hates crowds," said Jacob.

"Right."

Jacob and Abigail squatted down and lifted up the edges of the tablecloth. Sure enough, Brian and Ernest were happily settled back under the table eating huge pieces of wedding cake.

"Brian! You can't just wander away from us. We were frightened." It was the first time Abigail had spoken harshly to her father. "And Ernest, you should know better yourself. You're both naughty." Abigail was on a roll. "Stop eating that cake! You both need to have some decent food in your stomachs before you fill up on sugar. I don't want to have to look after two little boys out of their minds on sweets."

All three boys looked at Abigail with slack-jawed amazement.

"I'll stay here with these two while you go get some food from the buffet, Jacob. Get a big plateful and make sure it's food we like," commanded Abigail.

Dutifully Jacob headed over to the buffet. Sometimes it was better to just go along with Abigail, especially if she was in a mood—which seemed to be the case right now.

Being fairly indecisive by nature, Jacob was slow in choosing the sandwiches and pickles and cheeses and raw vegetables that eventually filled his plate. He was just reaching over to add some melon slices to top off his collection, when he heard a familiar voice speaking softly to him from behind.

"You've got some appetite today," said the voice.

"Um, yeah." Jacob turned around.

The eyes and the voice belonged to the ten-year-old girl in their first adventure; Aline was the same sweet, gentle person. Today, she was the mother of the groom.

"It's for my brother and my sister and my dad," explained Jacob.

"Children are always hungry."

"We definitely seem to be," said Jacob.

"Y'all related to the bride?" his great-grandmother asked.

"Yes," said Jacob, "And the groom, too."

Mema seemed puzzled by this.

"I'd better get back to the others," said Jacob.

"By all means," said Mema.

As Jacob turned to go, he felt a terrible tightening in his chest. It was the feeling that a child (or an adult) gets when someone who loves him very much gets brushed aside; when hurt is given and immediately forgiven. Jacob felt sure Mema didn't know who he was and he was just as sure she loved him, though she couldn't know why. Mema was the only one in the room who'd seen him and he felt sad he couldn't stay with her.

"You took so long!" Abigail accused Jacob when he crawled back under the table. "We have to eat and get out of here."

The four children quickly emptied the plate that Jacob had filled so carefully. When almost all the food was gone

—71—

(save two or three egg sandwiches), Abigail divided up the cake the smaller boys had started on earlier.

"I figured out how we arrived here," announced Abigail. "Look," and she pointed to the tablecloth in front of them, "that's the tablecloth Mommy uses at Christmas or when we have fancy guests. It must have been in the laundry."

"Oh no!" said Jacob. "We're going to have to get it off the table in the middle of the reception? How are we going to do that?"

"Grandpa will help us," announced Ernest.

"He can't do anything—he's the star of the party, he's the groom!" said Jacob.

"He's not the star. The bride is always the star," corrected Abigail.

"If we can get Grandpa away from everybody, I'm sure he'll see us, and then he can help us," said Ernest. "Follow me."

Ernest led the group, with Abigail carrying Brian, to just beside where Grandpa stood. Grandma was turned away, talking to people. Ernest grabbed hold of Grandpa's suit jacket and started to pull him away from Grandma and the wedding cake table.

"Where are we going?" whispered Abigail.

"I'm not sure. There must be a quiet place around here somewhere," Ernest whispered back.

The groom was wandering aimlessly around the room. Whenever someone stopped to talk to him, he

would edge away, not quickly and certainly not with purpose, but definitely away.

Some of the guests had seen the groom's mother talking to herself earlier and now the groom was drifting through the crowd in a most peculiar way. These guests wondered if Eva McCurdy really knew the family she was marrying into.

Finally Ernest led the group through a set of doors into a cloakroom. They were alone.

Grandpa looked a little queasy as his grandchildren and his son-in-law materialized in front of him.

"Grandpa, I'm your namesake, Ernest Wayne."

Grandpa looked even queasier. "I should've got to bed a whole lot earlier last night," Grandpa muttered to himself.

"Congratulations on your wedding," said Jacob. "How are you doing?"

The children stood solidly before him now.

"Who are you?" he asked, smiling at them affectionately but curiously.

"I'm Abigail, and this is Jacob and Ernest."

"Ernest Wayne," added Ernest.

"We're your grandchildren," said Jacob.

"You're all so good-looking," observed Grandpa.

"And this is your son-in-law, our father Brian." Abigail continued the introduction.

"Why is he younger than y'all then?" Grandpa asked, looking suspiciously at the baby.

"We're time travelling and we have to get him back to 1951. We need your help," said Abigail.

Grandpa looked at the three older children. "I'd do anything for you kids," he said.

"You always say that," said Jacob.

"I do?" questioned Grandpa.

"You spoil us," announced Ernest. "That's your job."

"I'm planning to be a geologist, but I suppose I could do both things," said Grandpa. "How can I help you?"

"We need the tablecloth under the wedding cake. We have to have it in order to get back to Toronto and then get Brian back to Nova Scotia. Nana is really going to miss him. Besides which, Baby Brian and grown-up Brian can't be in the same place," said Abigail, breathlessly.

"It makes Daddy stardusty," said Jacob.

"Oh," said Grandpa. He still seemed a bit guarded in his response to Brian, but that's often the way with sons-in-law.

"If you could get Grandma out of here, then the party would be over and we could take the tablecloth," said Abigail.

"You mean Eva?"

"Yes," said Abigail.

"The reception was supposed to end about an hour ago, but she loves to talk. I'd like to go on my honeymoon—our honeymoon," mused Grandpa.

"I guess Grandma's always loved to talk," said Jacob.

"Maybe we can just pull her out, like we did you," suggested Ernest.

"She wouldn't like it if I pulled her out, but I'm sure she'd love to meet you," said Grandpa.

"We may have to wait till later on to meet her. I'm worried about Daddy," said Abigail. "And Mommy too."

"I forgot you'd need a mother," said Grandpa, looking confused and slightly frightened for a moment.

"I don't mean to be rude, but let's go get Grandma and we'll have time to talk another time," said Abigail. She put Brian's sock and shoe back on his foot and picked him up.

"How'd you get to be so beautiful?" asked Grandpa.

Abigail just rolled her eyes, as she always did.

As usual, Ernest led the way. He suggested Grandpa wait by the doors, and then he went over to Grandma and grabbed a handful of her wedding dress. He then pulled her gradually through the crowd towards the door. Grandma was a little more difficult to manoeuvre because she kept talking to people along the way and resisted being pulled. But, eventually Ernest brought her over to Grandpa and handed her over.

"It's time to go," said Grandpa.

"I was having such a good conversation with Frank about..." began Grandma, but she stopped. Four children whom she had never seen before, but to whom she seemed irresistibly drawn, stood before her. The strange thing was, the children weren't exactly solid human beings, they were sort of half-way solid and half-way invisible.

Jacob reached out his hand to her, "Grandma," he said.

"Wayne?" Grandma turned to Grandpa.

"I want to start our honeymoon," said Grandpa.

"It's very unusual to have spirits at a Methodist wedding," said Grandma.

"I'll explain what I can on the drive to Niagara Falls," promised Grandpa as he led Grandma out of the room.

The reception guests followed right behind the couple, shouting good wishes and throwing rice.

Finally the room was almost empty and the children wasted no time sliding the tablecloth out from under the wedding cake. They each grabbed another piece of cake, and within seconds they were on their way home.

Chapter Six

Laughing Candies

Actually, they all weren't on their way home. There was a mix-up on the final "Apper dapper apper do!" and Jacob was left behind. He'd tripped on his own shoelace jumping up and down, and he fell away from the group. He landed on his elbow, and it hurt so much he couldn't help crying. The pain and the tears kept him from realizing, for a minute or so, that the others had left without him.

When he did notice he was alone in the room, he was very frightened. He forgot about the pain in his elbow, but he kept on crying.

The tablecloth was gone, and so were his father and his brother and sister. Nothing connected him to where he belonged. He was trapped.

The room was starting to fill up again. When some of the women noticed the tablecloth under the wedding cake was gone, they moved the cake over to the buffet table and collapsed the table it had been on. Jacob had to scramble to keep out of the way, but nobody noticed him, which set him off on another bout of weeping. He made his way over to a straight-backed chair at the end of the room. He dropped his head onto his hands.

He overheard someone say that the families of the bridal couple had all left; that meant he couldn't even talk to Mema. People were now cleaning up the room.

The thought that Abigail and Ernest would definitely come back for him was just forming in his mind when he felt a hand on his back.

"Who's your mother, little boy?" a woman's voice came from right above his head.

The thought of his mother back in Toronto, unconscious on her bedroom floor, not to mention over forty years in the future, drove any thought of rescue out of Jacob's mind and he was once again overcome with tears.

The woman pulled another straight-backed chair alongside Jacob's and spoke again. "Don't cry so, please."

Jacob noticed that standing up or sitting down, the voice came from almost the same place. He saw a small square-looking woman who might be somebody's grandmother. She wasn't his grandmother though or his great-grandmother or even an aunt; she was no one he'd ever seen before. She wore glasses covered in little tiny sparkles and a number of beaded necklaces rested on her shelf-like bosom. She looked sort of stern at first, but there was something about her, just beyond her eyes, that wasn't stern at all. In his mind he quickly leafed through all the photographs he could remember, and he definitely couldn't place this woman. Jacob's mind was moving very fast, "If she isn't a relative, why can she see me?" he thought.

"Who are you?" he blurted out, and then realized he must have sounded rude.

"I'm Hazel Finley. Who are you?"

"Jacob," he said. Jacob was thinking: Hazel, Hazel, Hazel. I don't know any Hazel. And then he blurted out: "I don't know you." (This was a lot of blurting for Jacob, but he really wasn't himself.)

Hazel looked a little taken aback at first, but she answered, "I don't know you either, but you seemed so upset. I hate to see a child upset."

Jacob looked at Hazel a little more intently, and he could see she didn't love him the way Mema had loved him when she didn't even know who he was, but nevertheless she seemed very kind.

"My family left without me," Jacob explained.

"They'll be back. Weddings can be confusing, and you don't seem like the kind of boy anybody would try to lose," comforted Hazel.

"I hope not," Jacob said. "Though I'll bet Abigail's thought about it."

"Your sister?"

"Yeah. And I have a brother, Ernest. I'm in the middle. I hate being in the middle. I do want them to come back though."

"They will," assured Hazel. "While we're waiting, I have something you might like."

"What is it?"

"Well, it's secret and kind of magical," said Hazel.

"Oh." Jacob sounded disappointed. "I'm actually kind of tired of magic."

"Really?"

"I don't mean to be rude," said Jacob. "Things have just been a little much lately."

"The great thing about this is that it's only as magic as you want it to be." Hazel opened up her pocketbook and pulled out a small tin container. She held it in the palm of her hand and took the lid off. "Laughing candies," announced Hazel.

"Laughing candies?" queried Jacob. They looked like perfectly ordinary lemon drops to him.

"Why don't you try one?" suggested Hazel.

"Well, I'm not supposed to take candy from strangers. But these aren't exactly ordinary circumstances: I'm lost in time, separated from my family and invisible to just about everyone," said Jacob.

"Now don't feel sorry for yourself, Jacob."

"I'm not. I guess I'll try one," said Jacob as he reached over and contemplated which one of the ten or twelve in the tin he wanted. They all looked the same. Eventually he chose one. Hazel took one too.

"So, Jacob. What do you call a bee that buzzes quietly?" asked Hazel.

"Pardon me?"

"What do you call a bee that buzzes quietly?"

"A bee that buzzes quietly? Hmm. That would be a mumble bee," answered Jacob.

"Good. Now, how do sailors get their clothes clean?" asked Hazel.

"Sailors? I don't know."

"They throw them overboard, and they're washed ashore," said Hazel, starting to giggle.

"Ugh!" said Jacob, but he said so feeling a little more relaxed.

"You tell one," suggested Hazel.

"All right. Three people are walking along under an umbrella, but none of them gets wet. Why?"

"It has to be because...because it isn't raining," said Hazel, fully laughing.

"Good for you," said Jacob. "Ask me another one." He was feeling a lot better.

"What are often served but never eaten?"

"Peas and corn?" asked Jacob.

"Tennis balls. Which room has no walls, no windows, no floor, no ceiling and no doors?"

"I know that," said Jacob, laughing now, "a mushroom. Knock, knock."

"Who's there?"

"Irish stew."

"Irish stew who?"

"Irish stew in the name of the law."

The laughing candies had done their magic; to those who could have seen them, both Jacob and Hazel appeared to be having the time of their lives. Jacob was, of course, invisible and Hazel had performed an act of sympathetic magic: her kindness made her barely visible and of no bother to the few remaining wedding guests.

"Hey, you're a regular mushroom yourself, Jacob," said Hazel.

"Oh, why is that?"

"You're a real fun guy. Hee hee," laughed Hazel.

"They *are* laughing candies," said Jacob. "Do you know why the dinosaur crossed the road?"

"To get to the other side?"

"No. Because chickens weren't invented yet," said Jacob, pausing for a moment. "I love stupid jokes."

"Me too," said Hazel. "The great part is that I always understand them." And she guffawed.

Jacob guffawed too and could barely get out the words: "Me, too."

Hazel and Jacob didn't notice the white, cloudlike object that appeared suddenly in the middle of the floor or the sharp thud that accompanied its arrival.

"Knock, knock," began Jacob.

"Who's there?" asked Hazel.

"Orange," said Jacob.

"Orange who?" asked Hazel.

"Jacob Lawrence!"

The laughter stopped.

Jacob and Hazel looked up to see Abigail, Ernest and Baby Brian wrapped up in the tablecloth like it was an oversized cape. Abigail was carrying Brian and she looked pretty upset.

"I've been worried sick about you, and here you are carrying on like a buffoon," snapped Abigail. "Mommy and Daddy are still unconscious and we have to take Brian back. Come on!"

"Hazel was just trying to cheer me up," said Jacob.

"Thank you," Abigail said politely to Hazel. "But we've got to go."

"Your parents are unconscious?" Hazel asked.

"Don't worry," said Ernest. "They'll be all right soon."

"Let's go back to the cloakroom. We need some privacy," said Abigail.

"Goodbye, Hazel," said Jacob. "Thanks."

"Goodbye, Jacob, children," responded Hazel, wondering if she should worry. She decided not to and put away the laughing candies for the next time they would be needed.

So, Jacob was rescued and the four children returned to Toronto together.

Chapter Seven

Tarifa

Their parents were, as Abigail had announced, still unconscious. Their mother looked more comfortable than she had before; she looked more asleep than unconscious. Their father was still stardusty, but he too looked peacefully asleep.

"Keep Baby Brian as far away from Daddy as you can," Abigail ordered her brothers. "Now, we need the baby sweater to get back to Nova Scotia, right?"

"He's wearing the sweater," said Jacob. "We just have to try again."

The children were very deliberate in their movements this time; they knew the hysteria of their last launching had got them off course. Abigail got into a laundry basket and Jacob handed her Brian. He then helped Ernest before climbing in himself.

The last words spoken before they started the "apper dapper apper do!" were Jacob's warning to Ernest: "Don't hang on to anything but Brian's sweater!"

But, how many four-year-olds do you know who

do exactly as they're told?

The children landed in sand, which was a great relief to all of them. It was an even greater relief when they looked up and saw an ocean.

"Thank goodness," said Abigail.

"Where's the bonfire?" asked Jacob.

"Don't be such a worrier, I'm sure it's right around here somewhere," said Abigail.

"I don't know. This doesn't really look like Nova Scotia," said Jacob.

"Now you're an expert on the place?" said Abigail, falling into sarcasm. But she knew Jacob was right.

Simultaneously, Abigail and Jacob cried out: "Ernest!"

"Things always go wrong with magic," answered Ernest cheerfully. "Remember *Half Magic*?"

"Sometimes you don't seem to know the difference between books and life, Ernest," said Abigail accusingly. "Where are we and how did we get here?"

"It's obvious how we got here. He was hanging on to something besides the sweater. What was it, Ernest?" demanded Jacob.

"I don't know," said Ernest. He wasn't cheerful any more. In fact, tears were starting to roll down his cheeks. He was sitting in the sand next to Brian, and the two little boys were holding hands.

"He doesn't want to take Brian back," surmised Jacob.

"We don't have a choice in the matter. Daddy's going to completely fade away if we don't return Baby Brian to his time and place. And who knows what else could happen. Ernest, do you know where we are?" asked Abigail.

"No," said Ernest. He and Brian were now holding both one another's hands.

"Which direction do you think we should walk?" asked Jacob.

"That way," said Ernest, gesturing to the left.

"All right, let's go," said Abigail. "Jacob, help get Brian on my back. You know Brian, having to carry you through time and history is exhausting. Why don't you learn to walk?"

"Walk?" asked Brian in his little baby voice. He slid down Abigail's back, landed on his feet and proceeded to take his first steps.

"Daddy's learned to walk! Daddy's learned to walk!" shouted Ernest, clapping his hands at the accomplishment.

"What a smart boy," said Abigail. "If only your sons would do just what *they're* told."

"Abigail!" said Jacob, impatiently.

The wind came up suddenly and started to push the children in the direction Ernest had indicated. They held one another's hands, Abigail and Jacob on the outside of the line and Ernest and Brian on the inside. The wind blew stronger and stronger, and the children felt that instead of walking along the beach, they were taking great long strides and bouncing like astronauts on the moon. It was a thrilling feeling, but also frightening (like the best of thrills) and they held on to one another very tightly.

There were no other people on the beach, no boats in the water and not a sign of life anywhere; just the children and the wind.

They blew and bounced along for a considerable distance. Finally, the children noticed three figures up ahead on the beach.

"Maybe those people can tell us where we are," suggested Abigail.

"We're invisible, remember?" said Jacob. "But we could hang around them and see if they give us any hints."

"We know them already," announced Ernest.

As he said this, the three figures ahead seemed to come into focus for the children.

"That's me! That's me!" shouted Abigail as she let go of Brian's hand and started to run ahead.

"Be careful Abigail. Remember Daddy!" warned Jacob.

"Daddy's here and Mommy too! Come on!" shouted Abigail.

"Abigail stop! It's dangerous," said Jacob.

Abigail didn't want to stop. She'd been so worried and upset about her parents that when she saw them upright and conscious, all she wanted to do was throw herself into their arms and feel safe again.

"Abigail!" Jacob didn't have to call again.

Abigail dropped to her knees in the sand. She was like a puppet that had suddenly lost its puppeteer. When the other children reached her, her brothers settled on either side and her father on her lap.

"Everything will be all right very soon," said Jacob in a soothing sort of voice. "But we have to be careful. I don't want you to get all stardusty, and I don't want Daddy to get stardusty all over again in the past."

"It isn't right that it's so dangerous," complained Abigail.

"The time travel seems to be okay as long as we don't meet up with ourselves," said Jacob. "It's unnatural for people to live in the past and present at the same time. I don't know about the future."

"Nobody knows about the future," said Abigail sullenly. "It isn't fair."

"You sure are cute," said Ernest, gesturing to the other Abigail on the beach.

The other Abigail was about the same age as Baby Brian. She was pouring sand back and forth between two buckets. Mommy and Daddy looked a lot younger, and what shocked their children was how relaxed they looked: sitting on the beach despite the wind, eating a baguette and drinking wine from a bottle. They were talking comfortably and laughing.

The children realized they must be in Spain, on a

beach outside Tarifa—the place where the Atlantic and the Mediterranean meet. Abigail and her parents had spent a winter there when she was a baby.

"What do we do now?" asked Abigail.

"We have to figure out what Ernest was hanging onto in the basket. Once we know what brought us here, we can get back to Toronto," said Jacob.

"That's not going to be easy," said Abigail.

"Yeah, we have to keep our distance," said Jacob. "We can't let Mommy and Daddy know we're here. We have to protect that Daddy."

"And we have to hurry before Abigail turns stardusty," said Ernest, thrilled (perversely so to his brother and sister) with the situation.

"I'm a menace to myself," said Abigail, with a heavy heart.

Baby Brian snuggled closer into Abigail's lap.

"We're going to have to act like spies," said Abigail, shifting her mood.

"Yeah," agreed Jacob.

"I'm a really good spy, Abigail," said Ernest.

Abigail looked at him out of the corner of her eye.

"Spy," said Brian.

"Everybody on your stomachs," ordered Abigail as she slid Brian off her lap and onto the sand. "We can't be spotted."

The children did as they were told. Brian was just starting to doze off when the group had to move. Daddy had scooped baby Abigail up into his arms and onto his shoulders, and the family of long ago were starting their walk back into town.

"Stay down!" commanded Abigail. "On your stomachs!"

"Do you want us to crawl into town, Abigail?" asked Ernest, imagining the possibility.

"Stay low!" reiterated Abigail. "They're turning around!"

"Mommy just dropped her shoe, it's all right," said Jacob.

"They're going to see us!" said Abigail.

"No, they aren't. They're talking to each other," said Jacob.

"Walk!" said Brian. And they did.

On their right, across the water, was Africa. On their left, the town of Tarifa came into view, edged by low apartment buildings.

When their parents reached a road leading north into town, the children followed. Our children observed two things that struck them as most un-Toronto-like: the first was that the streets were filled with children playing games: ball games, skipping games, doll games. Every child in Tarifa was outside, and every parent was somewhere else. Sure, there were adults on the street, but they seemed entirely disconnected from the children. The children were free.

The second unfamiliar thing the children noticed was the laundry: it was everywhere. Laundry hung from

apartment buildings, was draped across rooftops and wafted in the breezes of patios and ruins. Laundry hung from almost every available space in town; it too was free.

By chance, Abigail glanced three floors up to some lines of laundry hanging in a narrow corridor between two apartment buildings, "That's it," she said to the others. "What we're looking for."

"Mommy's blouse," said Ernest. "I really didn't mean to touch it."

"We'll grab it and then get out of here," said Jacob.

Our children followed their family around the corner into a nondescript apartment building.

"I feel kind of funny," said Abigail.

"You'd better stay down here," said Jacob. "Ernest, you and Brian look after Abigail."

Abigail sat down on the stairway, Ernest and Brian beside her. Jacob slipped past them and ran up to the third floor, where he could hear a woman firing machine-gun-like Spanish at his mother. He had no idea what she was saying; he knew his mother probably didn't understand either.

"Are you feeling stardusty, Abigail?" asked Ernest.

"I just feel a little weak," said Abigail.

"Try and move your hands through each other, like Daddy did," said Ernest.

"Ernest, don't be morbid," said Abigail. "Brian and I need a nap."

"There's a spot under the stairs where you could curl up," suggested Ernest.

Within minutes both Abigail and Brian were sound asleep, and Ernest was their invisible sentry. It was quiet in the hallways now, and Ernest wondered how Jacob was doing upstairs.

All of a sudden there was another blast of rapid-fire Spanish coming from upstairs. Then a door slammed and someone was rushing down the stairs. The footsteps stopped almost at the bottom of the stairs and sobs began, broken only by the sound of a match being struck to light a cigarette.

Abigail and Brian remained asleep, but Ernest was curious. He poked his head around the corner and saw a youngish-looking woman with dark wild hair, sobbing and smoking. She looked directly at him.

"*Que pasa, Niño?*" the woman said.

"You can see me?" asked Ernest.

"Of course, I can see you. I see everything," the woman said. "I'm desperately unhappy."

"You speak English," noticed Ernest.

"My heart is broken," announced the woman.

Ernest looked at her carefully, and she did look like

she had a broken heart: her eyes were red and swollen from crying, and she didn't look like she could smile, no matter how many sweets she was offered.

"Do you know the people upstairs?" asked Ernest, hoping to change the subject.

"The Canadians?"

"Yes."

"Happy people only remind me of my own unhappiness," she said, dramatically flicking ash from her cigarette onto the steps below. "Do you know Garcia Lorca?"

"No, we're just visiting," said Ernest.

"The great Spanish poet." And she began to recite.

Black are the horses.
The horseshoes are black.
On the dark capes glisten
stains of ink and of wax.
Their skulls are leaden,
which is why they don't weep.
With their patent-leather souls
they come down the street.

"*The Ballad of the Spanish Civil Guard*," she said as she ground her cigarette out.

"I like books about dogs and magic and vehicles, but mostly whatever anybody will read me," said Ernest.

"I read to help me cry," said the woman.

"It doesn't seem like you need much help. What's your name?" asked Ernest.

"Esperanza. And yours?"

"Ernest. Would you like to meet my dad?"

"Most adults lack empathy. I don't think so," said Esperanza, lighting another cigarette.

"Oh, he isn't an adult now. I want to keep him as a baby, but my sister won't let me," explained Ernest. "He's right over here, napping. Brian!"

Ernest roused Baby Brian from his nap. Most babies are unhappy when awoken, and Brian was no exception. Perhaps he was expecting to find himself in a carriage on a beach in Nova Scotia, gently woken by his mother and comforted by her. Instead, he was brought to consciousness on a cold, tiled floor under a stairway in Spain, and attempts to comfort him were made by his youngest son, who was then three years older than he was. Brian cried, loudly and with conviction.

"Oh, no, don't cry," said Ernest. "I just want to be with you. Come and meet Esperanza." Ernest brought Brian out from under the stairway and up to where Esperanza sat, but Brian cried even louder.

"Wah! Wah!" he cried, tears flowing freely and his little body stiff with unhappiness.

"Oh, please don't cry!" Ernest was starting to get agitated himself. "He really likes me. I don't know why he's crying so much."

"Maybe he's hungry," suggested Esperanza.

"No, we were just at a wedding and we had lots to eat," said Ernest.

Brian continued to cry.

"He's probably overtired then. Here, let me hold him," said Esperanza.

"You can't smoke around a baby," said Ernest with authority, shielding Brian from her.

"I won't smoke. I'll try to calm him down," responded Esperanza. She stamped out the second cigarette and took Brian from Ernest. She juggled Brian up and down and back and forth in the space just inside the front door.

Abigail slept.

"He's not crying so loud," observed Ernest.

And Brian wasn't. Esperanza kept jiggling Brian, and his sobs grew less intense. Ernest, without thinking, starting mirroring Esperanza's movements. The two of them moving up and down and back and forth as if synchronized. Eventually Baby Brian stopped crying.

"Shh," said Esperanza, as she jiggled Brian back to sleep.

Ernest and Esperanza continued their gentle dance without speaking while Brian slept.

Eventually Esperanza could no longer contain her curiosity: "You say this is your father?"

Meanwhile, Jacob had just managed to get hold of the blouse—and it hadn't been easy. He'd slipped into his family's apartment while his mother had been out in the hall with her neighbour. He spotted the washing machine right away in the centre of the kitchen, and the laundry hung out from a window beside it. He hid in the pantry until he was certain his sister and parents had settled into their siestas.

Jacob finally felt that everyone was probably asleep; he heard three distinctive sounds of snoring.

His mother's blouse was not right outside the window on the line, which meant that Jacob had to bring in a lot of other laundry before he reached what he needed. Jacob knew that before he opened the window. What Jacob didn't know was that after a few towels on the line and before the blouse were a number of very large bedsheets twisting and snapping in the ever-more ferocious wind. A gale-force wind.

Remember that Jacob was seven years old and though tall for his age, was not tall enough to reach the clothesline without standing on a chair. And, standing on a chair to lean out of a third floor window in gale-force winds to wrestle sheets off the line and drag them in—well, Jacob's palms got very clammy with anxiety.

Jacob dropped a lot of clothespins. It disturbed him that it took so long to hear them hit the ground.

At one point, the chair started to slip out from under him and Jacob had to throw himself onto the kitchen floor to keep from being tossed out the window.

When he finally had his hands on the blouse they'd spotted from below, Jacob lay down on the floor to catch his breath.

"This is really laundry in the extreme," thought Jacob as he lay in the midst of the crispest, brightest and freshest smelling laundry he'd ever experienced. He often rested in clean laundry, but Spanish laundry was ambrosia: the smell of the sea in the sheets and towels was so intoxicating that Jacob lay there for some time. The rest (his siesta) revitalized him, and by the time he got up, he'd completely forgotten his ordeal at the window. Needless to say, he left the laundry in the middle of the kitchen floor, a state of chaos not yet the norm for his parents' household.

He snuck out the door with the blouse under his arm, and as he descended the stairs he heard an unfamiliar voice speaking English.

"I suppose it's true," Jacob heard. "If I can calm a crying baby, I can do anything. I can go back to Madrid and I can live my life. Ernest, yes, I can live my life!"

As he made his way down the last flight of stairs to where Ernest and the woman stood, the woman didn't seem to notice Jacob.

"Did you get the blouse?" Ernest asked him.

"It's right here," said Jacob. "Where's Abigail?"

The woman looked at Jacob myopically.

"Esperanza, this is my brother Jacob. Jacob, this is Esperanza," said Ernest.

"Were you upset, Ernest?" asked Jacob.

"No, why?" asked Ernest. "Brian was crying, and so was Esperanza."

"I was desperately unhappy, but I don't feel it quite so intensely now," said Esperanza.

Jacob thought about this for a minute. Hazel had seen him when he was unhappy, and Esperanza had seen Ernest when she was unhappy. What did it mean? He couldn't spend a lot of time pondering the question because he again remembered his sister.

"Where's Abigail?" he repeated.

"She's asleep under the stairs," said Ernest. "I'll wake her up." He moved over to where Abigail was and suddenly let out a blood-curdling scream, "Arraaaagh!", just like the screams his parents had made back in Toronto all those pages ago.

"What is it?" said Jacob, rushing over to where Ernest stood. He didn't scream, but he was horrified.

Abigail was even more stardusty than their father had been. Perhaps her age had made her more sensitive to the dangers of being with one's past self. At this point, she looked more like a planetarium star show than a human being: speckles of stardust congregating in the barely recognizable shape of a little girl.

"We've got to get out of here right away," declared Jacob.

"We can't move her," said Ernest. "There's nothing to grab on to."

"We'll just have to crowd around her. Can you hand me Brian, please?" said Jacob to Esperanza.

Esperanza gently placed the sleeping Brian in Jacob's arms.

"Do you need some help?" she asked.

"No, but we do need privacy, I think," said Jacob. "Thank you."

"Goodbye Ernest," said Esperanza. "Don't ever allow yourself to become too unhappy." And she started back up the stairs, back to where she'd come from.

Jacob gave Ernest the blouse to hold onto and with Brian half asleep in Jacob's arms, the two boys grabbed at handfuls of Abigail's stardust and gently tried to apper dapper apper do the group back to Toronto.

Chapter Eight

The Sidecar Ride

When Jacob, Ernest and Baby Brian popped back up in the laundry basket in Toronto, they were relieved to discover Abigail's stardust had accompanied them from Spain. What used to be Abigail was now a shimmering, glittering mass of tiny particles barely retaining Abigail's shape.

Jacob and Ernest looked over the edge of the laundry basket to see their father's flickering shape on the bed. Their mother still lay unconscious on the floor.

Jacob grabbed the blouse from Ernest and threw it as far as possible out of the basket. He then handed Brian over to Ernest and warned grimly: "Don't touch anything but his sweater!"

Sombrely they chanted: "Apper dapper apper do! Apper dapper apper do!" And they were on their way.

This time they absolutely, positively had to get it right. So they did. They landed on the same sand dune they'd landed on what felt like months ago. The bonfire was burning down, but it was there, just steps away from the same ocean in which they'd been skinny dipping. There was no doubt, this was Nova Scotia.

Jacob felt an immense sense of relief, until he looked down and saw Abigail: stardust sprinkled on the sand. A wave of fear washed over him, and he froze, immobile.

Without really being aware of it, Ernest knew just what to do. He grabbed a couple of empty Coke bottles left by the fire and filled them with seawater.

"Salt water's good for just about anything," he said as he poured water over Abigail's stardust. He splashed some water onto his brother too; Ernest knew Jacob needed rousing nearly as much as Abigail.

"Oohhhh!" sighed Abigail, the sound of her coming back before the sight of her. Pretty soon she started to materialize and as she did, she spoke.

"I have such a headache. I feel like I've been flattened by a road paver or maybe struck down by a terrible disease or forced to do long division in my head. What's 652 divided by nine?"

"Seventy-two with four remaining," answered Jacob, returning to normal.

"Abig!" shouted Brian as he jumped on top of Abigail.

"Uggh!" said Abigail, hugging her father and tickling him, happy to be whole again. "Where are we?"

"Nova Scotia," answered Jacob.

"That's great," said Abigail. "We'd better put Brian

back in the carriage and wait for Nana to come for him."

Ernest grabbed hold of Brian's arm. "No," he said, "I don't want to give him back."

"We have to give him back," said Jacob.

"No, we don't," countered Ernest.

"Ernest, how can you be so great about some things and such a nincompoop about others?" asked Abigail.

"I'm a human being," answered Ernest. "I want to be with Brian."

"You are, in Toronto," said Jacob.

"A baby brother is different from a dad. Maybe we can stay here with him and Nana can look after us," suggested Ernest.

"No, that would change everything," said Abigail. "We need to be with Mommy and Daddy."

"This *is* Daddy," argued Ernest.

"No," said Abigail.

Ernest started to cry. Brian looked confused, then started to cry himself. Jacob looked distressed. After all, he loved big Brian and Baby Brian too. Abigail, fortunately, had recuperated enough from her stardusty state to take charge of the situation.

Abigail circled the fire in search of the carriage. She had gone around twice when Ernest announced: "The carriage is gone!"

"Oh no!" cried Abigail.

"Nana probably thinks he's been kidnapped," said Jacob.

"He was kidnapped! We kidnapped him! What are we going to do now?" Abigail looked hopeless, her take-charge attitude melted like a popsicle dropped on the sidewalk on a hot day.

"The decision's been made then. We take Brian back with us. We move to near the ocean so Daddy can swim in salt water every day and everyone will be just fine," announced Ernest.

"Stop it Ernest! You're just making it worse for everyone," said Jacob. "We're taking Brian back to Nana with no ands, ifs or buts. The big problem is finding out where Nana lives."

Abigail and Jacob sat down on the beach beside Ernest and Brian. Abigail had a faraway look in her eyes.

"Now that Brian is back in his own time, is he invisible like us or not?" she mused.

"We have no way of knowing until we meet up with somebody else," answered Jacob.

"This has sure been a long day," sighed Abigail.

"We'd better get going," said Jacob.

Ernest and Brian had buried their legs in the sand and Jacob had to dig them out.

"Come on, Abigail, snap to," said Jacob.

"After this is all over, I don't think we should apper dapper apper do any more," said Abigail.

"I'm not going to stop," said Ernest.

"Let's talk about this later," said Jacob.

"Talk," said Brian.

But, instead they walked. Without any energy, the children trudged up the hill behind the bonfire. Over the crest of the hill, the town was laid out before them. It was a bit of a shock to see cars and pedestrians and stores right there, like Roncesvalles on a Saturday afternoon (or like what Roncesvalles might have been over forty years ago). They hadn't heard any sound but the ocean while they'd been on the beach, and at the edge of town, it was almost as if the beach didn't exist. The two worlds seemed completely separate.

"I don't know where to begin," said Abigail.

"There's a post office just up the street. We could start there," suggested Jacob.

"We're not going to send her a letter," said Abigail.

"I know. I was thinking maybe..." but Jacob was interrupted by a very loud "WOW!" from Ernest.

"WOW!" he said again.

Abigail and Jacob looked behind them to where Ernest was looking. At first they saw nothing, though they heard a motor. The motor was coming toward them from behind the same sand dune they had just crossed. Suddenly it appeared over the top, and they could all see a motorcycle, with a sidecar attached. Inside the sidecar, a small, nervous woman was jerking her head from side to side as if she were scouring the landscape for something or someone.

"Nana!" the three older children blurted out at once.

She didn't hear them, and she didn't see them.

"She can't see Brian," said Jacob. "He's invisible now too."

"That shouldn't matter. He's her son, and we're her grandchildren," said Abigail. "Everybody else saw us."

"She looks pretty scared," said Jacob. "Fear makes people blind to things."

"And she's with the policeman," said Ernest.

The motorcycle and sidecar came to a screeching halt in front of the coffee shop a block away. Abigail picked up Brian and they rushed across the street and down to the coffee shop. Nana looked even more pale close-up. The policeman had climbed off his motorcycle and was helping Nana out of the sidecar.

"You could use a cup of tea now, Ma'am," said the policeman.

Nana's colour started to return once she was standing on solid ground. "I'm going to have to tell my husband," she murmured to herself, and then she directed her attention to the policeman. "Why would a kidnapper kidnap *my* baby? What do you think happened, Constable Vincent?"

"I don't know, Ma'am," said Constable Vincent as he led Nana into the coffee shop.

"Mama!" called Brian after her.

"Quick," urged Abigail. "Help me get Brian into the sidecar."

"Don't you think we should just take Brian in to Nana?" asked Jacob.

"It might cause too much of a stir. Nana is already terribly upset," said Abigail. "This is better."

"What if he stays invisible?" Jacob asked.

"I don't think he will," said Abigail.

"I want to ride in the sidecar too," interrupted Ernest.

"Not now, we've got to get Brian back to Nana," said Abigail.

"I want a turn!" insisted Ernest.

"Stop it!" barked Jacob.

Abigail and Jacob started to settle Brian into the sidecar.

"Dernest!" said Brian.

"Shhh!" said Abigail.

"Gee, there's no seat belt in this thing. No wonder Nana was so shaken up after her ride," said Jacob.

"How are we going to get their attention?" asked Abigail.

"Squeeze the horn," suggested Jacob as he gestured to a chrome horn with a big red rubber squeeze-it ball on the handlebars.

"Stand back, everybody," warned Abigail as she squeezed.

"OONNNKK!" sounded the horn.

Constable Vincent rushed out of the coffee shop.

Ernest jumped into the sidecar.

The constable examined the motorcycle from all angles. He saw nothing.

The children noticed Ernest in the sidecar.

"Ernest!" shrieked Jacob.

Abigail and Jacob started to pull Ernest out of the sidecar.

Constable Vincent shrugged his shoulders and went back into the coffee shop.

"You've got to stay away from Brian, or nobody will be able to see him," scolded Abigail.

Ernest started to cry. "I want to ride in that sidecar."

"Let's try again," said Jacob, "I'll hold Ernest back." Jacob pinioned Ernest's arms from the rear while Abigail squeezed the horn again.

"OONNNKK!" sounded the horn.

This time Constable Vincent rushed to the door of the coffee shop. From where he stood, it looked for a moment as if there was something inside the sidecar, something small just peeking over the edge. He took a step forward, and whatever it was disappeared, POP, like an optical illusion. He returned inside.

Ernest had, of course, wrestled his way free of Jacob's arms and leapt into the sidecar a split-second after the policeman appeared. Abigail and Jacob started to haul their brother out of the sidecar yet again when they realized that Ernest was so stubborn that he was going to have to have that ride. In fact, when they thought about it (for at least a second), Abigail and Jacob were eager to ride in the sidecar themselves. They climbed into the sidecar with Ernest and Brian to discuss the matter. It was crowded, a little like inside a laundry basket.

"Okay," announced Abigail, "We'll go for one quick spin around town, and then Brian has to go back to Nana and we have to get back to Toronto. Agreed?"

"Agreed," said Jacob. "Brian? Ernest?"

Brian clapped his hands.

"How about a long spin?" pleaded Ernest.

"We can make the adults in our life a little crazy—after all, we can't help it. But we shouldn't make them really crazy. That's mean," said Abigail.

"I don't want to be mean, I just want to have fun," said Ernest.

"I know," said Abigail. "This can be our last special time with Baby Brian, right?" She hugged her father close.

"Kids," said Brian.

"Everybody ready?" Abigail squeezed the big rubber ball again.

"OONNNKK!" sounded the horn.

Constable Vincent quickly appeared at the door to the coffee shop. Nana was beside him.

"This is extremely suspicious," said the constable.

"I think I'd better go home," said Nana. "The kidnappers may be trying to get in touch with me."

"I'll give you a lift," offered the constable.

"No!" insisted Nana. "I want to walk."

Nana didn't move though. She stood staring at the sidecar. Her eyes were blank and empty, as if her fear had blinded her.

All four children instinctively leaned closer to Nana to comfort her, but they could make no difference to her now. They felt sad and guilty that they had Brian and even guiltier at leaving her for the sake of a ride in the sidecar. But, being children, they made the choice for pleasure.

"We won't be long," Abigail voiced what they all knew had to be true.

"I'm going to take another tour of the beach in case we missed any clues. I'll stop by your place afterwards, Ma'am," said Constable Vincent.

"Yes," said Nana absently as she turned and walked away.

The constable revved his motorcycle.

"Here we go!" said Jacob, who sympathized with his Nana's fear, but still wanted that ride.

The motorcycle and sidecar sped away from the curb and up the street before it crossed over to the sand hills. As the vehicle hit the sand, Ernest stood up and yelled out, "Yiipppee!"

Abigail, Jacob and Brian all reached for him and pulled him down lower in the sidecar. The constable stuck his finger in his ear. The vehicle bounced along the beach, and the Toronto children recognized the spot where they'd been swimming—it seemed like years ago.

They drove a long way up the beach, zigzagging through the sand and scrub grasses. If there was a baby Moses to be found along this shoreline, he would have been found: Constable Vincent was a thorough detective. Eventually the beach turned rocky and the motorcycle/sidecar had to turn back.

For the children, the ride was marvelous, fantastic. In the noise and the motion of the sidecar, Ernest and Brian clutched each other and pointed out birds and waves and clouds and piles of driftwood along the beach. Jacob hung on to the edge of the sidecar so tightly his fingernails were blue-white, the fear an utter thrill. Abigail loved the jolting twists and turns and started to imagine a poem to describe the ride.

The children had all concentrated on their ride so much that they had ignored the driver. He was muttering to himself, though the sound of the motor drowned out his words. Abigail studied his lips moving and thought he said: "A baby doesn't disappear into thin air. He's got to be here somewhere."

As the vehicle approached the remains of the bonfire again, a sodden mass of something lay washed up on the beach in front of them. When the constable noticed it (a few moments after the children), he gasped. As they got closer, the children recognized the clothes they'd lost when they'd gone swimming. The constable stopped the motorcycle and got off to investigate. He gingerly laid out each set of clothes on the beach, fitting the right shirt with the right pants by size, adding the socks and underwear. When he had three sets of clothes in order, he got out a notebook and wrote down (mouthing the words as he did so): "One boy, approximately aged four. Another boy, approximately aged seven. One girl, probably nine or ten years old." He stopped and sighed. His eyes seemed to fill with tears. "Three more children," he said.

A chill ran through each and every child in the sidecar. Even Baby Brian looked at the constable with concern. In that moment, our children finally understood (if only temporarily) adult worries and distress. "What are we going to do?" asked Jacob.

"Hang on. It's almost over," said Abigail.

"We have to take our laundry back to Toronto. It's the only way they'll forget about us here," said Ernest.

Constable Vincent gathered up the clothes, folding everything neatly and stacking it into the sidecar. The clothes were damp and fishy-smelling; they definitely added to the discomfort of the children crowded into the sidecar. All in all, the adventure had turned sour.

During the ride back into town and through the

streets to Nana's house, the children were glum. Ernest and Brian seemed reconciled to parting. Jacob gagged a few times and almost threw up from the fish smell, and Abigail suddenly missed Mommy and Daddy.

Nana's house was a perfect little clapboard cottage with a front porch. Nana was sitting on the porch when the motorcycle pulled up in front. Heavily, the constable dismounted and moved to join her.

"Quick," ordered Abigail, "take the wet clothes and put them behind that tree over there."

"I don't want to touch those stinky things," said Jacob.

"Then help Brian out of the sidecar," said Abigail, as she grabbed the wet clothes and raced across the street to hide them.

"What are we going to do about the constable?" Jacob asked Abigail when she returned.

"He'll either see us or he won't," said Ernest. "He will see Brian."

All four children stood on the grass in front of Nana's house. The constable was talking to Nana.

"Now, are you sure you don't know three children, aged four, seven and ten—two boys and a girl, Ma'am? Let me show you these clothes and see if they ring a bell. Maybe some neighbourhood kids," he said.

Nana and Constable Vincent had just stepped off

the porch. The children could see that Nana didn't want to look at the clothes. She was wringing her hands and breathing shallowly.

All of a sudden, Brian started running toward his mother. She couldn't see him, but she felt him grab onto her leg. As soon as she felt him, he became visible to her. And then to Constable Vincent as well.

"Mama!" Brian cried.

"Brian!" Nana cried as she scooped him up and into her arms. "You're walking and you're talking! My baby!"

"Is he all right?" the constable asked.

Nana held Brian out from her body for a moment and then hugged him tightly again. "He looks just fine," she said.

"But where did he come from? The street is empty," said the constable.

"Kids," said Brian.

"Did he say 'kids'?" asked the constable.

"I can't believe he's talking. The only word he knew before was 'hi'," said Nana.

"Brian, I want you to look at these clothes and tell us if you recognize them," said Constable Vincent as he moved toward the sidecar.

"He's just a baby," insisted Nana.

"Kids," said Brian.

"Oh, my goodness!" said the constable. "They're gone!"

"Who's gone?" asked Nana.

"The clothes. I left them right here," said the constable. "There are too many suspicious things about this case."

"But the case is closed," said Nana. "I have my baby back."

"I'm off to the station to check the missing persons reports. You're going to have to make a statement, Ma'am. I'll be back later," said Constable Vincent as he positioned himself on the motorcycle. "There's too much mystery here for my liking," he said as he sped away.

"Mama," said Brian.

"Brian," said Nana.

"Down," said Brian.

Nana lowered Brian to the ground, and he ran over to where his children stood. "Kids," he said.

Gradually three children, just as the policeman had described them, materialized beside Brian. Nana felt very confused and a little woozy as the children appeared, but despite this uneasiness she seemed very drawn to them, as she could see Brian obviously was.

Abigail had decided not to tell Nana who they were. After all, Nana had been through a lot, and she looked exhausted. "We just want you to know that nothing bad happened to Brian," Abigail began.

"Dernest," Brian interrupted, as if to introduce his son.

"Are you the kidnappers?" asked Nana without any anger.

"Yes," said Jacob. "We're sorry."

"Goodness," replied Nana, warmly, as if she rather liked these children who admitted to being kidnappers.

"We want to say goodbye to Brian," said Abigail. "We have to go."

Jacob moved to kiss Brian on the cheek, as did Abigail. "Goodbye," they both said. "We love you." Brian patted each of them on the back in a very Brian-like gesture.

Ernest reached for Brian's hand. "I'm going to miss you, but I know you belong with Nana," he said.

"Nana?" said Nana.

"Oh, Dernest," said Brian.

"He said his first sentence," noted Abigail.

"Make sure you tell Constable Vincent we're all right," said Jacob to Nana. "We don't want him thinking that we've drowned."

"Let's go," said Abigail. "Oh, we need the sweater to get us back." She peeled off Brian's sweater, giving him one last kiss.

The children then stepped away from their father and their Nana and crossed the street to pick up the wet clothes. They decided to walk a little further up the block out of sight to do their time travelling. They waved to Brian and Nana as they walked away, and they could hear a little voice call out: "Apper dapper apper do!"

"Now he's talking in complete sentences," commented Abigail.

"Yeah," her brothers replied wistfully.

And they were on their way.

Chapter Nine

The Three Little Kittens

On the trip back from 1951, the children hoped their father would be completely well again, now that Baby Brian was back where he belonged. But on their return, they found him as stardusty as ever, and their mother was still unconscious on the floor.

"What do we do now?" asked Abigail as she crawled out of the laundry basket over to her mother. She noticed that her mother had a little dribble of saliva coming out of the side of her mouth, and Abigail used the edge of her cuff to wipe it away. Abigail knew her mother wouldn't like to look undignified, even when she was unconscious. Her mother sniffed a little, but didn't wake up.

"We need sea water," said Ernest.

"You mean we have to go back to Spain or Nova Scotia and bring back a jar full of sea water?" asked Jacob anxiously.

"I'm sure Mommy has some sea salt in the kitchen cupboard. We could mix up some of our own," suggested Abigail.

"No," replied Ernest, "I'm pretty sure it has to be real sea water."

"Where do you get these ideas?" asked Jacob, feeling short-tempered and queasy from travelling back to Toronto clutching their still-wet stinky clothes.

"I don't know," said Ernest. "It's what worked for Abigail, though."

"That's true. I just don't like the idea of apper dapper apper doing again. I don't want to leave Mommy and Daddy again," said Abigail.

"Speaking of which," she continued, "I think we should swear a vow of secrecy. I don't think Mommy and Daddy are up to hearing about our adventures."

"I don't like the idea of keeping a secret from them," objected Jacob.

"Oh, don't be such a goody two-shoes, Jacob. They'll never be up to understanding what happened to us, and you know it," insisted Abigail. "You know how helpless Mommy and Daddy are. I mean, look at them!"

"They're unconscious!" protested Jacob.

"That's true, but even at the best of times they seem totally confused by life. We have to protect them," said Abigail.

"I don't want to swear," said Jacob.

"I do," said Ernest.

"We just have to make a pact then. Let's use this," said Abigail as she grabbed a book from a pile beside the bed. The book was *The Lion, the Witch and the Wardrobe.*

"I'm not sure Aslan would want us to make this pact," said Jacob.

"Stop it!" said Abigail. "He's a character in a book."

"Who's to say he isn't as real as you or I?" asked Jacob.

"The point is not who's real, the point is that we have to keep a secret," corrected Abigail, a little condescendingly.

"Jacob, Abigail's right for once," said Ernest.

"Gee, thanks a lot Ernest," said Abigail.

"I don't know," ruminated Jacob.

"Okay then, repeat after me: we vow to keep our Apper Dapper Apper Do Adventures secret from Mommy and Daddy," said Abigail solemnly.

"And from anybody else too," added Jacob.

"Yeah, we don't want the whole world finding out," said Ernest.

"All right, from everybody," agreed Abigail, but then she added, "in our time."

"In our time?" puzzled Jacob.

"We've already told Grandpa. We should make a pact that we can keep," reasoned Abigail. Her brother assented, and the three children each put a hand on top of the book and made their vows.

Their mother started to stir.

"I know what to do," said Ernest. He picked up the

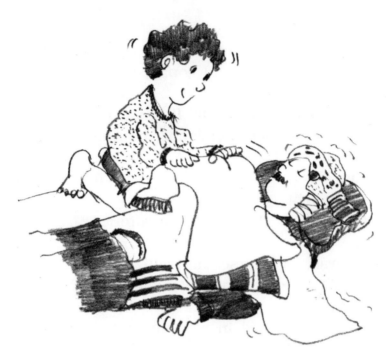

pile of wet clothes the constable had found on the beach. "There's got to be enough sea water in these to bring Daddy back."

"Are you going to squeeze them out?" asked Jacob, trying to suppress a gag.

"No, we'll just lay them over Mommy and Daddy like this," said Ernest as he draped some very stinky socks across his father's stardusty forehead. He continued draping shirts and socks and underwear and pants across his father's body.

The pungent saltwater and fish smell drove Jacob from the room. He sat in the bathroom, hoping he wouldn't be sick.

Abigail draped the remaining garments over her mother, who snorted and coughed and then sat bolt upright.

"Ugh! What is that smell? It must be the meringue! Wait a minute, I don't remember putting the pie in the oven. Brian?"

It was a relief to see her mother fully conscious, Abigail thought.

"Brian? Brian?" her mother continued. "Are you all right?"

Brian was, of course, all right. He had returned, without fanfare, to complete solidity. Ernest stood beside him.

"Why am I covered in wet stinky clothes, Ernest?" asked his father.

"To make you feel better," Ernest answered.

"You know, I think it's worked. I do feel better," he said. "Now I need a shower." Brian got up from the bed, and all the wet smelly clothes fell on to the floor. "After I have my shower," he continued, speaking to their mother, "I'll start the laundry."

"Good," she answered. "And I'll finish the pie."

The parents proceeded with their plans. Abigail and Ernest were flabbergasted. Why were they so matter-of-fact about the smelly laundry? Had their mother forgotten about the baby? Did their father even notice he'd been stardusty?

Jacob was no longer fighting nausea in the bathroom;

he was now taking refuge in his bedroom. Abigail and Ernest tracked him down.

"They don't seem to have any idea what happened," said Abigail. "And they're not even curious. I don't understand it at all. Maybe it's the magic."

"We're going to have pie," said Ernest.

"Why am I thinking of the three little kittens?" asked Jacob.

"Meow, meow, meow," said Abigail with a twinkle in her eye. Ernest joined in the last "Meow".

And so the children had their pie and went to bed, voluntarily, right after dinner. Our three were very tired and barely needed their sleepytime comforts: the glasses of water, bedside chats and treasures hidden inside and under pillowcases, usually so necessary at bedtime. The excitement of the day dimmed very quickly for all concerned.

This willingness to go to bed was a little bewildering to the parents, but then the ease with which the parents had been revived was bewildering to the children. Yet both generations soon shrugged off their puzzling botherations and went on with their lives.

Chapter Ten

The Red King's Sash

Life was very busy in the days and weeks that followed that eventful Saturday. It was nearing Christmas, and the children were so busy they didn't even think of time travelling. They played boarding school (The Narnian School for Kings and Queens with Abigail as Queen Susan, the imperious headmistress) and pirates (with Ernest once and for all allowed to be the pirate captain) and sock-skated through the house (until Jacob fell and hurt his head on the kitchen floor). They skulked around the basement looking for hidden Christmas presents. They had large groups of friends over who ran up and down all the stairs in the house, screaming and giggling in the inevitable war between boys and girls.

Abigail, Jacob and Ernest also had rehearsals for *The Christmas Story*, which was performed every year at The Church of the Holy Trinity, the old, old church right behind The Eaton Centre. Abigail always played an angel, which pleased her because she got to wear a lot of make-up. The boys were always shepherds, which suited them because their mother was a shepherd too. Ernest had been the Baby Jesus one year, but that was a one-shot deal. The rehearsals and eventual performances took a lot of time and kept everyone's imagination occupied.

After the last performance of *The Christmas Story*, Susan, the director, asked members of the cast for volunteers to launder costumes.

"We will!" piped up Abigail.

"Abigail," said her mother under her breath, "you know I have enough trouble keeping track of our own laundry. I don't think I can take responsibility for costumes."

"I'll take responsibility, Mommy," assured Abigail.

"Well, all right then. If it's something you want to do," said her mother, drifting off to help lay out the pot-luck dinner.

"Why do you want the costumes, Abigail?" asked Jacob.

"Just think, *The Christmas Story* has been performed here since 1938. Some of these costumes are really old. I think we could have a pretty good (and safe) adventure because we wouldn't risk meeting up with ourselves," explained Abigail.

"You mean we wouldn't use the family laundry anymore?" asked Jacob.

"Right, we could really go out into the world," said Abigail.

"I thought you didn't want any more adventures, Abigail," said Ernest.

"Well, now I think I do."

"Me too!" said Ernest.

"Let's face it," said Abigail, "the laundry magic isn't going to take us as far back as Babylon or prehistoric Ireland. It's a magic of things in our world."

"Hazel and Esperanza were all right," said Jacob, thinking about the kind strangers in their last adventure, "but what if we meet some really bad people? I mean, isn't that what Mommy and Daddy are afraid of?"

"There are no guarantees, Jacob. We could have got into a lot more trouble last time out, but we didn't. I want to see what else we can see; I want more adventures," said Abigail.

"That's why we have the magic, Jacob," said Ernest, earnestly.

"Well, I suppose after all the excitement of Christmas dies down," said Jacob, "it might be good to have something to do."

"Hurray!" shouted Ernest, as he ran off to grab a handful of corn chips from the buffet.

It wasn't until weeks later that the children remembered their plan. Their father had returned to work after his Christmas holidays and their mother was completely absorbed by *The Enchanted Castle*, which had actually been Abigail's present. The children knew they could disappear (as was their plan) and their mother would never notice.

The costumes had been washed and folded and returned to the bag and left in a corner of their parents' bedroom—to be forgotten until about mid-May. Abigail had not, in the end, been the one to do this laundry. Her mother had done it in a sort of frenzy on Boxing Day, while the rest of the family played with their gifts. Therefore, the children didn't really know what was in the bag of costumes, and the first order of business was to see if there was anything of obvious interest. They dumped out the bag onto their parents' bed.

"All shepherds' costumes," said Abigail, clearly disappointed.

"What's wrong with shepherds?" asked Jacob.

"There's nothing wrong with shepherds as people, Jacob. It's just that the way they dress is boring. The colours are boring, the styles are boring and the stories in the clothes are probably boring," explained Abigail. "I was hoping for something with a little more pizzazz."

"Hey, look at this!" cried Ernest. He pulled a shimmering something out of the bottom of the bag.

"What is it?" Jacob asked.

Abigail grabbed it out of Ernest's hand. "It's the Red King's sash. It must have got into this bag by mistake," she said.

"It's beautiful," said Jacob. And sure enough, it was. The sash (or belt) was red satin with silver cord and jewels. The children knew that neither the silver nor the jewels were real, but it was still dazzling.

"This is where we need to go!" announced Abigail.

"Wow, do you think we'll go back to medieval times?" asked Ernest.

"No, if this was from medieval times," answered Jacob logically, "then it would be in a museum somewhere, not in a bag of costumes."

"It does look old though, Jacob," said Abigail.

"We won't know where we're going until we get there," said Ernest cheerfully.

"Are you sure we can't try a shepherd's costume?" asked Jacob.

"No," said Abigail definitely, "let's go!"

And so the children crowded into an empty laundry basket, and Ernest hung onto the Red King's sash while the three jumped up and down and chanted "Apper dapper apper do! Apper dapper apper do!"

As they felt themselves depart, they heard their mother shout from the living room below: "Stop that thumping!" So they did.

The landing was extremely hard and dark and damp and cold. Wherever they were, it smelled really yucky, like the creepiest part of their own basement, which made them realize they probably *were* in a basement.

"Oh no," said Ernest.

"Shh!" said Abigail.

"What a mistake!" said Jacob.

"Shh!" repeated Abigail.

"I can't move, Abigail!" protested Ernest.

"SHHUSH!"

None of them could move. They were trapped in a very small space, only slightly bigger than the laundry basket. Cold, hard things pressed against them and rattled when they moved.

"Abigail," Jacob whispered, "what are we going to do?"

"I don't know," Abigail answered.

Just then the children heard muffled footsteps on the other side of a door. The door opened and a hand pulled a chain attached to a light bulb above them.

As soon as the light was on, they all felt a little foolish to discover themselves wedged between shelves of preserves: jams and jellies and chutneys and canned vegetables—just like their mother made every summer and fall. They should have recognized the feel of the jars, but they hadn't.

The person attached to the hand was a girl of about nineteen, with short red hair and pale, pale blue eyes. She was very thin and her skin was grey and tired-looking (the bare light bulb was most unflattering). She was wearing a work dress and an apron and heavy stockings with very ugly shoes. She didn't see our children in the cupboard, and they had to squish out of the way so she wouldn't step on them as she moved to examine jars and put them into a basket hanging over her arm. She sighed in a tired kind of way.

Ernest was the first to slither past her and out the door. Jacob and Abigail quickly followed, crawling awkwardly over the girl's black old-lady shoes. Fortunately, the girl didn't feel a thing. She did, however, sigh a few more times.

The basement before them was very large, much larger than their own.

"This must be a mansion," said Abigail, shivering. "I think that was a servant."

"Cinderella," suggested Ernest.

"I don't think so," said Jacob. "Let's go upstairs. I don't want to get locked down here again."

"This way," said Ernest, leading the others up a curved set of stairs.

The children entered a spotless and decidedly old-fashioned kitchen. It was a large room with a long table in the centre. On the table were two trays: one with a collection of Bunnykin plates and bowls and cups and the other with two crystal wine glasses and a cut-glass bottle filled with a pale liquid.

"At least there are children here," whispered Jacob.

"Let's hope," whispered Abigail in response.

Ernest moved over to the icebox: a large oak cupboard with a big brass handle and hinges.

"Don't touch anything!" warned Jacob.

"It's an old-fashioned refrigerator," said Ernest, as he opened the door. "Look," he said, and the others moved closer. The icebox was completely empty except for a bowl full of water and a little chunk of ice.

"I wonder what they eat," said Ernest.

"They eat ice," said Jacob.

"Shut the door!" ordered Abigail, as she heard footsteps on the stairs. The children scrambled to the edge of the room as the servant girl entered from the basement.

The girl (her name is Millicent, as we find out just a few pages further on) set her basket on the table and pulled out two jars, one of peas and the other of jam. She opened each jar with a POP to break the vacuum and she emptied some peas and some jam into the Bunnykin bowls. She then opened a cupboard and took out a hunk of bread, so hard and stale she had to chip it into three pieces with the point of a knife. She filled a pitcher with water from the tap and arranged everything on the children's tray. Finally, Millicent sighed heavily as she lifted the tray and left the kitchen.

Abigail, Jacob and Ernest just looked at one another until Ernest blurted out: "Who is she going to feed that to?"

"We'd better find out," said Jacob.

"It's so peculiar," said Abigail. "I mean, look at this house."

And they did. They looked through the kitchen door into an enormous formal dining room, filled with very fancy furniture.

"You'd think they would be rich," Abigail continued, as she led her brothers into the dining room for a better look. The children circled round the table, amazed at the opulence around them.

"It's just like Casa Loma," suggested Jacob.

"Similar," agreed Abigail.

From the dining room, our children could see across the entrance hall and into an elaborately furnished living room, with velvet curtains, chairs and couches, a big fireplace and above it, a painting of a beautiful young woman in a ball gown.

The painting, or rather the woman in the painting, looked like a goddess or an angel, she was so lovely. Her skin glowed from the inside, like a candle burning behind thick milky glass. Her eyes were clear and green, and she had a calm, serene expression as if she knew she was divinely beautiful. Her dress was cardinal red and it took our children a few moments— they were hypnotized by her beauty—to recognize the Red King's sash loosely tied around her waist.

"Ahh," said Abigail, leading her brothers into the living room. The painting and its subject fascinated them. Our children stood together, silently gazing at the portrait for some time.

They didn't hear the doorbell ring, but all of a sudden

there were voices in the entrance hall.

"You'd better hurry, your bath'll be getting cold. SimSim, you go first tonight."

"Oh, no. Do I have to have a bath again?" said a boy's voice.

"Your tea's set out, so hurry on."

"We had so much fun in the park, Millicent," said a young girl's voice. "People were feeding the ducks and they let us join them."

"It's not the ducks that need the food," said Millicent, harshly. Then she changed her tone. "Hurry on up now. Your parents should be home soon and I have to figure out what to do with them."

"Are we going to see them tonight?" asked another girl's voice.

"I don't know how their day's been," said Millicent. "Now, scoot upstairs."

The new children passed in front of the doorway to the living room. Our children could see a boy about Abigail's age and two girls, roughly the same age and size as Jacob and Ernest. Our children set out to follow them.

The staircase leading to the second floor was very wide and grand, and the first three children had no idea they were being followed by another three. This gave our children the opportunity to study their leaders from the rear. Each child was wearing a navy blue blazer, and the boy grey shorts and the girls grey skirts. Their socks all matched, and their shoes looked fairly new. Both girls had blond ringlets like Shirley Temple. They all looked very well put together; not like children who survived on little more than bread and water.

When the first three children reached the top of the stairway, they turned to their right. The smallest girl absentmindedly looked behind her and let out a cry: "Oh!"

Involuntarily, Abigail let out a cry: "Ah!"

The older girl then looked behind her and her cry was: "My!"

Jacob stepped forward. "Don't be frightened," he said.

"We're here for a visit," added Ernest.

The boy did not turn around, but kept on walking. "Quiet!" he said. "Wait until we're in the nursery."

The five others obeyed. They followed the boy down the hall and up another, much narrower, set of stairs. Finally they reached the nursery and the door was shut.

"Who are you?" the older girl blurted out.

"Whimsy, don't be rude," ordered the boy.

"But SimSim, they're dressed so strangely and... Oh, I'm sorry," she said, catching herself.

"I'm Abigail and these are my brothers, Jacob and Ernest."

"We're time travelling," piped in Ernest.

"Goodness," said the younger girl as she stepped closer to Ernest and looked him up and down.

Ernest spread out his hands, as if presenting himself to take a curtain call. He forgot to bow.

The older boy studied Ernest for a moment, then said to Abigail, "I saw you in the living room, under Mimsy's portrait."

"Mimsy?" queried Abigail.

"Our mother," answered the boy.

"I'm surprised that you can see us," said Jacob.

"But you're standing right in front of us," said the older girl. "I don't understand."

"Time travel," answered Jacob. "It's got a logic of its own, and we're just learning how it works. I mean, it's surprising that you can see us, because we're not related."

The three new children looked confused.

Jacob continued, "And no one here's a baby. None of us is truly unhappy, at least not today." He paused. "Oh, then you must be unhappy. That's why."

"I'm not sure how to answer that," said the boy, a little startled.

"We're fine," said the older girl. "We just try not to think too much."

"Did Millicent see you?" asked the younger girl.

"No," said Abigail.

"But she's unhappy almost all the time," said the younger girl.

"I think her unhappiness is a habit. I wouldn't say it's true," said the older girl. "We should introduce ourselves: I'm Whimsy and this is my brother SimSim and my sister Rosebud."

"Those are your real names?" asked Ernest.

"Well, no," said the boy. "Our real names are Simon, Winnifred and Rebecca. The others are names our parents call us. Endearments, I suppose."

"Your parents must be very playful to give you those nicknames," said Abigail encouragingly.

"Playful?" asked Simon, "No." He sounded very much like Eeyore, Winnie the Pooh's melancholy donkey friend.

"They say the names will keep us cheerful," said Winnifred.

"And do they?" asked Abigail.

"No," said Simon, again sounding very Eeyore-like, then shifting. "You know, I think I'd like to try what it's like to be Simon for a while. Call me Simon, please."

"And we could be Winnifred and Rebecca," said Rebecca to her sister excitedly.

"What can you tell us about time travel?" asked Winnifred.

"We're from Toronto, 1999," announced Ernest.

"No!" said Rebecca, her green eyes widening.

"Where are you?" Ernest asked Rebecca.

"Toronto, 1938," said Rebecca.

The children all looked at one another in amazement.

"It's like E. Nesbit," said Winnifred.

"You read her too?" asked Abigail.

"Every one," said Simon. "So, what do you use for the time travel: an amulet or a carpet, or do you have a Psammead?" He didn't wait for an answer. "And what's the future like? Will our fortunes be restored? Did you come to help us?"

"It would be so good of you to help us," said Winnifred. "Mimsy and Papa go out every day to look for money, but they haven't found any. Do you know where it is?" asked Rebecca.

"No," said Abigail. "We don't really know anything about money. I'm sorry."

"Why did you come then?" asked Simon, his momentary cheerfulness slipping away.

"The Red King's sash," said Ernest.

"Are you connected with royalty in the future?" asked Winnifred.

"No," said Jacob quickly, not wanting the conversation to go off the rails again so soon.

Simon's interest rallied. "What is the future like?"

"Well," said Abigail, hoping to please, "You can read E. Nesbit and lots of other wonderful books... "

"*The Mennyms*," Ernest interjected.

"Yes, you can read anything you want. And, adults are free, at least I think so, but children aren't," continued Abigail.

"I don't understand," said Winnifred.

"She means that we can travel through time by

ourselves, but we can't go to Roncesvalles without an adult," said Jacob.

"Roncesvalles? Why that's just a few blocks over," said Rebecca.

"Where's your house?" asked Abigail.

"High Park Boulevard. We go to the park every day," said Winnifred.

"By yourselves?" said Ernest, "Wow!"

"Everyone else is far too busy to come with us," said Simon.

"Millicent has to look after the house, and Mimsy and Papa have to look for money," said Rebecca.

At this point, all six children settled their attention on the table with the tray of Bunnykin dishes and the food upon the dishes.

"Please," gestured Winnifred, "be our guests. There isn't much, but what we have we can divide."

An awkwardness settled on the children. They were all embarrassed. No one knew what to say.

Finally Ernest broke the silence, "Why don't we go out!"

"Yes, let's go out," agreed Rebecca.

"Rebecca!" said Simon, sternly.

Abigail had been fidgeting in the awkwardness, and suddenly she discovered that she had her change purse in her pocket. Inside the sparkly plastic were nickels and dimes and even a looney and a tooney.

"Look," she said, "I have some money. Why don't you be our guests?"

"That's very kind," said Winnifred shyly.

Simon was wary. "I don't know."

"We could walk up to Caufield's Dairy and then buy some fruit at Carpento's Fruit Store. It wouldn't be expensive," Winnifred continued.

"What's that?" asked Rebecca, pointing at the money Abigail spilled into her palm and held out for the others to see.

"That's a looney. It's worth a dollar and that's a tooney, it's worth two. You can't use them for another sixty years, but here, why don't you take them?" said Abigail.

"Gee, thank you," said Rebecca.

"We can't restore your fortune," said Abigail apologetically, "but we can have a little fun. And fun is good."

Jacob looked at the other children earnestly and agreed, "Fun is good."

"Please, SimSim, please, can we go to Roncesvalles?" Rebecca pleaded.

"Well, we do sneak out sometimes, and I don't think anyone ever notices," said Simon. "There's a fire ladder out the nursery window."

"A fire ladder! Now this is an adventure!" enthused Ernest.

"I remember reading about the Sunnyside Amusement Park," said Abigail.

"Oh yes, let's go there!" suggested Rebecca.

"You can't go anywhere dressed like that, though. We'll have to get you blazers so you don't look quite so unusual," said Simon.

"But we're invisible," said Jacob, suddenly realizing the complications of an outing.

"Pardon me?" said Simon.

"Well, we're visible to you, obviously. But we're not visible to everyone," said Jacob. "Millicent didn't see us, and if we go out into public, it might get sort of ticklish: being seen, not being seen, you talking to lamp posts—the whole thing."

"Gee, I hadn't thought of that," said Abigail.

"I think your clothes would make us visible," said Ernest, solving the problem easily.

"Do I really have to wear a blazer?" asked Abigail, who was very fussy about her fashion statements.

"Mimsy and Papa insist we wear the children's uniform," said Winnifred. "We need to keep up appearances, always."

"But at an amusement park?" Abigail asked no one in particular.

Simon went into the next room to get the needed clothes. Jacob decided to test the jam—after all, he was a connoisseur of condiments. He picked up a spoon and scooped up some of what appeared to be apricot or peach preserves.

"Wow, this is good," he said, helping himself to another spoonful.

"We have peach trees in the garden. Millicent makes wonderful jam," explained Rebecca.

"It's great," said Jacob, as he sat down to finish the bowl of jam. He didn't bother with the peas.

"Sometimes he is so disgusting," said Abigail as she turned away from her brother.

Ernest decided he would test the peas. He ate one.

"Oh," said Abigail, suddenly remembering, "we need the sash your mother was wearing in her portrait."

"The Red King's sash," said Ernest, mashing peas between his fingers.

"I don't understand," said Winnifred.

"We need it to get back to 1999. It's what brought us here," said Abigail.

"I wish you'd take us back with you. I'd love to have an adventure," gushed Rebecca.

"We got into a lot of difficulty taking someone back with us once," said Abigail.

"Our dad," interrupted Ernest, scraping pea mash off his fingers with a spoon.

"It isn't safe," added Jacob, licking the last of the jam off his spoon.

"How disappointing," said Rebecca.

"We should get that sash now," said Abigail to Winnifred, "and then we'll have it for when we need it."

"I don't think Mimsy will be pleased. She's so particular about things," said Winnifred.

"It's the only way that we can get back home," said

Abigail, starting to feel a little nervous that Winnifred would not give up the sash.

"Everything has to be just so," said Winnifred.

"I'm sorry," said Abigail.

"Everything will be just fine as soon as we're back in 1999," said Ernest.

"That's true," said Jacob. "I hadn't thought of that, but all the laundry items from the past must get replaced in order for them to make it to the future. Your mother may not even notice it's gone."

"She probably won't," agreed Rebecca. "But if she does..."

"It would be most unpleasant," interrupted Winnifred.

"Your mother is really beautiful," said Abigail, trying to redirect the conversation.

"She says that great beauty is a burden. I think Papa would agree. Come on, I'll show you Mimsy's closet," said Winnifred as she led Abigail out of the nursery.

Simon reentered the room and Jacob and Ernest, who'd never worn anything like a blazer before, struggled into their new finery.

It took Abigail and Winnifred about thirty seconds to find the sash. All Winnifred's mother's clothes were arranged by colour in a closet the size of Abigail's bedroom at home. Most of the clothes looked as if they'd never been worn.

Winnifred looked small and plain standing in the

centre of the closet. "Mimsy takes very good care of her clothes," she said.

"Goodness," said Abigail, feeling sad and overwhelmed by the closet and the clothes and the orderliness and the extravagance. She took Winnifred's hand. "Come on," she said.

When the girls returned to the nursery, they noticed that Simon looked uncharacteristically cheerful. This was, of course, more obvious to Winnifred, who knew him better. But even Abigail noticed a lightening in his face, as if an encumbrance had been cast away. Jacob had been telling Simon the plot of a book he'd recently read, a book that wouldn't be written for almost sixty years. This prompted Simon to tell the others: "The future just goes on and on. Books get written, life continues."

"Believe in the future," added Ernest genially.

"Yes. And let's have fun," said Simon.

Winnifred smiled at Abigail. "Let's have fun."

"Hear, hear!" said Rebecca.

Abigail wore the sash under her blazer and the six uniformly blazered children slipped out the nursery window and down two flights of a fire ladder onto the lawn below.

In the sunlight, our children noticed the emerald brightness of the other children's eyes, as if they'd come more alive, somehow, outside their house.

The escapees started on their way.

Chapter Eleven

Freedom: The Golden Ring

When the children left Toronto 1999, it had been January: grey and cold and bleak outside, but in Toronto 1938, it was spring. The air felt brisk, and the light was bright and full of promise.

"What's the date today?" asked Abigail.

"April 17th," said Simon. "It should be light for another hour or so. We're always home by dark, we have to be responsible."

"Of course," said Abigail.

Jacob suddenly remembered the splendiferous feeling of listening to Charlie Pride while riding in their Grandpa's truck along the freeways circling Calgary. It was like the feeling he was having now: he felt free.

As the group approached the corner of Roncesvalles and High Park Boulevard, they could see the brick gates which signalled entrance to the Boulevard. The gates still stood in 1999.

Just then, a big black car approached the intersection and, without slowing down, turned onto High Park Boulevard.

"Mimsy and Papa," whispered Winnifred.

A handsome man, obviously a gentleman, was driving and beside him was a woman wearing a large hat, a scarf around her neck and sunglasses. She held a handkerchief trailing out the window like a signal flag, though the message was unclear. Neither the woman nor the man noticed the children on the sidewalk. And they were gone.

"Gosh," said Ernest, saying the only thing that could be said.

The children scurried across to the east side of Roncesvalles and started walking north to the dairy. A breeze from the lake picked up sounds from the amusement park, and the children could clearly hear the tinny music of the carousel as they walked along. These gay sounds were broken shortly by the clang and clatter of a passing streetcar. It was the kind of streetcar now reserved for sightseeing tours of Toronto: boxy and small and looking more like a toy than a vehicle to our children.

"Stop!" Abigail ordered the group. "I need to readjust this sash, it's falling down." And she wiggled around inside her blazer and tightened the sash around her waist. The end of it drooped below her blazer and the jewels sparkled in the early evening sunlight. As she fussed, she complained: "That sound drives me crazy."

"The streetcar noise?" questioned Jacob.

"No, silly," she said impatiently, "the carousel music.

I want to go right now and ride the carousel. I feel like I'm being hypnotized."

"It does make you want to be there," agreed Winnifred.

"We need something to eat first," said Simon.

"There's cotton candy at Sunnyside, remember Simon?" said Rebecca.

"We can't have cotton candy for food, we'll all throw up," said Simon, shocked.

"Cotton candy! Cotton candy! Cotton candy!" Ernest started chanting and Rebecca and Winnifred and Jacob and even Abigail joined in, right on the corner of Westminister and Roncesvalles. The desire for pleasure captured everyone except Simon, who was embarrassed and admonished them to "Stop!"

They didn't.

"Cotton candy! Cotton candy! Cotton candy!" they continued.

"All right!" relented Simon and he turned and led the group south down Roncesvalles.

"Cotton candy! Cotton candy! Cotton candy!" they continued.

"Enough!" ordered Simon, smiling finally.

Abigail, Jacob, Ernest, Winnifred and Rebecca stopped their chant.

"Everyone calm down," Simon

insisted. "Winnifred, recite a poem."

"All right," agreed Winnifred. And this was her poem:

Roncesvalles Lovers

Constance Fermanagh and Geoffrey Wright
    took a stroll down Roncesvalles
    one summer night,

The outing was grand as he held her hand and
    hummed a tune of love.
    Ta da!
    He hummed a tune of love.

They were on their way to Sunnyside Beach to a
    carousel ride and within their reach:
    the golden ring.
    Ta da!
    The golden ring to catch.

But at the corner of Fern, there stood a gal
    with a steely-eyed stare
    and a "Don't you dare!" snarling
    through her teeth.

It was Marion Galley, once young and sweet
    now mad as hell and twice as fleet,
    she nabbed Geoff Wright on sight
    and knocked him off his feet.

"You ill-got brute, you knavish swine
    I am your puppy and you are mine.
    You sowed my Garden and you will reap
    my flowers, my weeds, my berries and
    burrs—NOT HERS!

"Now she goes home and we go down
    to Sunnyside Beach and Palais Royale
    to dance,
    without Constance,
    the night away."

So, Constance Fermanagh went home alone and
    Marion Galley and Geoffrey Wright
    rambled down the Avenue hand in hand:
    Roncesvalles lovers
    on a summer night.

"Millicent made it up," explained Rebecca. "She tells us stories in the evenings."

"She's very inventive," added Simon. "Does someone tell you stories, Abigail?"

But Abigail had started to skip ahead as soon as the poem was finished. She was anxious to get to the carousel, and the others followed suit.

Very soon the six children were standing before the carousel at Sunnyside Amusement Park. It was a beautiful carousel with brightly painted horses and regal carriages for those who didn't want to ride a horse. Mirrors in gilded frames were hung around the middle and at the top. The tinny music was so much louder and so much more hypnotic than it had been on Roncesvalles.

"I want to ride it," announced Abigail. "Now."

"I want my cotton candy first," said Ernest.

"Me too," said Jacob.

"Look, there's the golden ring," said Abigail as she pointed to a glittering band hanging from the roof of the carousel.

"It isn't really gold," said Simon.

"Sure it is, look at how it shines," said Abigail. She handed some change to Jacob. "Here, go get the candy. I'm going for a ride first. I hope the attendant doesn't notice this nickel is from 1993."

The five children turned to find a cotton candy vendor, and Abigail got on the carousel.

"If it isn't gold, what is it then?" asked Jacob.

"Brass," said Winnifred.

"I don't think she cares," said Ernest.

Abigail hadn't been on a carousel since she was very little, so this felt like her first time. She chose a particularly beautiful horse with violet feathers on his halter and golden decorations painted on his pure white mane. She called him "Lightning" to herself. The first few times she went round, Abigail simply took pleasure in the movement of the horse: up and down, up and down, so gracefully.

She looked out beyond the carousel to the amusement park. She could see a huge roller coaster labelled "Flyer" and another sign that read "Honey Dew", and she puzzled over what kind of ride that could be. She saw young couples and kids and men in suits and men in shabby clothes.

When she turned her attention back to the carousel, she again spotted the golden ring. And she wanted it. Abigail felt fairly certain that she would be tall enough to reach it if the horse were up instead of down as it passed by the ring. Every second time around, the horse was up. Abigail kicked off her shoes to prepare to stand. All of a sudden, it seemed, the ride slowed down and then stopped. It was over.

Abigail stayed on her horse and paid the attendant another nickel, this time from 1991. As she waited for the ride to begin again, a crowd of five or six boys about her age got on the carousel. They were loud and rough-looking and they used a lot of nasty words: words that she would never even think of using. The boys made Abigail nervous, until she thought of the golden ring and any thought of those boys went right out of her mind.

The carousel ride started up again. The others had found their cotton candy and were savouring every mouthful of fluff that melted into grainy sugar on their tongues: heavenly sweets. They had made their way back to the carousel to eat their confections; Abigail on the carousel was only a peripheral interest. That was, until Winnifred let out a cry.

"OH!"

The others looked up.

"She's standing on the horse!"

"What is she doing?"

"She wants that ring!"

"I didn't think she was really serious."

"I think she's going to get it!"

"Oh no!"

"The sash!"

"Those boys, they've grabbed it!"

"We've got your jewels now! La-di-da!"

And the tough boys leapt off the carousel, sash in hand, and darted behind a small pavilion.

"We've got to get that sash back!" screamed Jacob, who immediately ran after the boys. Simon followed.

Abigail didn't know what had happened. Winnifred, Rebecca and Ernest jumped onto the carousel and wove through the moving horses to Abigail. After all, the ride had only begun.

Winnifred and Rebecca each took hold of one of Abigail's shoes and tried to slip them on her feet. All the while their target moved up and down, up and down, and refused to cooperate. Abigail wanted one more try at the golden ring, and she couldn't understand why they were preventing her. Ernest tried to talk to her, but the tinny music seemed to get louder and louder, and it was impossible to hear anything but the nightmarish carnival melody. When the ride was over, Abigail was spitting mad.

"What are you trying to do to me? I have every right..."

Ernest interrupted her. "Some kids grabbed the sash when you were standing up."

Ernest didn't have to say any more. Abigail quickly tied her shoes and hopped off the horse.

"Which way did they go?" she asked when they were all well clear of the carousel.

"Behind there and toward the roller coaster," said Ernest.

"Simon and Jacob went after them," added Rebecca.

"They'll need our help," said Ernest.

And they certainly did. The tough boys had run circles round some of the food pavilions and smaller rides, all the while taunting their pursuers with the sash.

"We've got your jewels, now ain't we grand? Your la-di-da-di precious jewels!"

"They're not real jewels," called Simon.

"Now who's to say what's real or not? She wears the gear, she thinks she is the brass. You posh are all the same."

"Posh?" said Jacob, feeling quite confused.

The tough boys took off again, fanning out and

throwing the sash to one another as they raced toward the roller coaster.

Abigail and the others caught up to Simon and Jacob and joined in the chase.

"Everybody choose one kid to follow," suggested Ernest.

"He's right," said Simon, breathlessly. "Do the best you can."

The tough kids led the blazered kids under the roller coaster. They darted in and out among the wooden support frames, all the while tossing the sash back and forth. They moved so fast, Rebecca couldn't keep up with her boy, and then the others fell behind too. The tough kids moved like magic, slipping in and out of sight. The only thing that marked them was their voices: they taunted our children ferociously, and they used expressions no one had ever heard before.

At one point, Winnifred turned to Abigail and asked: "What does that mean?"

But Abigail didn't hear her because the roller coaster had started up overhead, and the clatter of the wheels and the screaming of the passengers blocked out every other sound. In fact, below the roller coaster the sound felt just like an earthquake, or so Jacob thought.

Ernest noticed that the tough boys suddenly seemed easier to follow; they were losing energy and interest. Everyone was uncomfortable below the roller coaster. One of the boys ran ahead toward the beach. Everyone else fell in behind him.

The beach was spotted with a few couples and bicycle riders taking a rest. One of the boys ran ahead with the sash and stopped right at the water's edge. He grabbed an end and spun it round his head, then hurled it into the water.

"Swim for your precious jewels!" he yelled out, and the others laughed as they sauntered off back to the amusement park.

The sash floated on the water and the fading sun reflected off the jewels like magic. That the sash didn't sink *was,* of course, magic.

Jacob quickly took off his blazer and his pants while Abigail tried to stop him.

"You get too cold. I'll do it," she said, slipping out of her blazer. "I hope it's not too polluted here."

"No," insisted Jacob, "I can get it." And with that, he dove into the water and swam out to grab the sash. When he had it, he held it up above his head like a hero with a trophy, which is how he felt.

"He looks so proud," said Winnifred.

"I hope the pollution doesn't make him sick," said Abigail.

"What pollution?" asked Simon.

"You know, all the chemicals and garbage people put in the lake. The water's dangerous," said Abigail.

"What do you mean? People swim here all the time," said Winnifred.

"Not in 1999. Ernest fell in once, but no one ever swims," explained Abigail.

"Well, maybe the lake can be restored. Perhaps people will swim in it again," said Simon, hopefully.

"It would be nice," said Abigail, noting Simon's optimism.

Meanwhile, Jacob had finally reached the shore. He'd held the sash above the water all the way in, so it had taken him longer to swim back.

Ernest and Rebecca met him at the water's edge.

"You were really brave, Jacob," said Ernest.

"Here are your clothes," Rebecca said.

The other children moved over to where Jacob stood. Abigail could see he looked cold and his teeth started to chatter. Ernest put the blazer around his shoulders.

Then, Jacob locked his teeth together for a moment and something passed across his eyes. He didn't look cold any longer. He started to talk: "I didn't have time to be afraid. I didn't have time to think about what would happen to us if we really lost the sash. Everything happened so quickly. There wasn't any time to think. I had to act without making a decision."

"But you've done that before," said Ernest. "When Daddy got stardusty and when Abigail was."

"I didn't pay attention then. Now I know that I can do it," said Jacob. "I am brave." He started to get dressed, pulling his pants over his wet underwear.

"Congratulations," said Simon.

"Are you cold?" asked Abigail.

"No," said Jacob. "I feel really good. How about you all?"

"We're just fine," said Winnifred, who looked extremely tired. "I wish our problems could be solved by something I could do."

Simon moved over to stand beside his sister, "It's all right, Whimsy. Some situations have simpler solutions than others. Our time will come. And we'll be as brave as Jacob."

"I can't help wishing you could help us," said Winnifred. "Or Mimsy and Papa. I guess I don't understand this time travelling."

"But, Whimsy," said Rebecca, "we had an adventure. We had fun and got to eat some cotton candy."

"This light isn't going to last much longer. We should probably start home," Simon warned his sisters as he started to move.

"You'll want to see your mother and father," suggested Abigail.

"We won't see them until tomorrow," said Winnifred.

"They probably have plans," explained Rebecca.

Abigail couldn't imagine what kind of plans these would be. "Why are parents so peculiar?" she asked.

The others looked at her, perplexed.

"Our parents aren't peculiar," said Jacob.

"Oh, come on Jacob, yes they are. They get confused. They often don't seem to know what to do," insisted Abigail.

"You always say that, Abigail," complained Jacob.

"They *are* helpless, sometimes," said Simon, catching Winnifred's glum mood. "And the worst part is, they know it. Every day they're less and less like people whose fortunes are going to be restored."

"Come on, Simon. E. Nesbit always has a happy ending," said Abigail.

"That's true," said Simon, recovering himself. "I'm going to believe in the future. Whimsy, I want you to believe in the future too."

Winnifred looked around the group, "All right," she said, "I will believe. What else can I do?"

"We have adventures and books and our parents have us," suggested Ernest cheerfully.

"Yes," agreed Winnifred.

"And we have friends now too," said Rebecca.

"I want my cotton candy," Abigail felt suddenly hungry. And so the children walked back to the amusement park to buy some.

"Those boys sure were bad," said Jacob.

"Really bad," agreed Ernest, relishing the thought.

"If only they knew how posh we're not," said Rebecca, laughing.

"It's true: appearances are deceiving," said Simon.

"But we keep them up," said Winnifred, brushing sand off her blazer.

"I wonder what their stories are, the tough kids I mean," said Abigail.

"Will you come back to visit us?" Rebecca asked Abigail.

"We could, if you want us to," said Abigail.

"Yes, we do. It would be too sad to say goodbye," said Simon.

"Then let's not say goodbye," suggested Ernest.

"But come back and surprise us anytime," said Rebecca.

"It would be something to look forward to," said Simon, testing out his newfound optimism. "Right, Whimsy?"

"It's Winnifred. And yes," said Winnifred.

Ernest and Rebecca stood side by side, very close together for a moment, like small children sometimes do, pleasantly pressed against one another's shoulder.

And then Abigail had her cotton candy in her hand. Jacob and Ernest both crowded in and tried to grab a piece for themselves and Abigail got mad. "Stop it! You had your own! It isn't fair to take mine!"

There was a short but noisy skirmish over Abigail's cotton candy, and when our three children looked up, the other three children had disappeared.

"We should go after them," suggested Jacob.

"No," said Ernest, "let's surprise them soon."

Our children turned inward towards each other once again.

"I want one more ride on that carousel," said Abigail. "I want another chance at the golden ring."

"It isn't gold," said Jacob.

"I want it anyway. Come on. Here's a dime for your fares, and I'll pay in pennies," Abigail said as she led them over to the carousel. "I want Lightning. You can choose any other horse."

Jacob and Ernest chose horses just behind Abigail's. They knew they had to keep an eye on her. Just before the carousel started to move, Jacob leapt off his horse and hurried over to Abigail.

"If you're planning to do anything crazy, you'd better give me the sash," he said. And she did.

Abigail didn't waste any time. She kicked off her shoes right away and stood up on Lightning's back. On the third time past the golden ring, Abigail managed to grab it.

"It's mine! I've got the golden ring! It's mine!" she shouted to her brothers.

Jacob was tempted to shout back at her: "It isn't gold, it's brass." But he didn't. She was too happy.

When the ride was over, Abigail let each of her brothers hold the ring, momentarily. It had already picked up warmth from Abigail's hand. For an instant, she wondered if the ring were magical: would it take her to the Wood between the Worlds? And then, instinctively, she knew it had no magic properties and she didn't care. She loved the ring for other reasons which she couldn't easily put into words. It reminded her of feeling free, the true gift of their adventures.

"I guess we need to find a private place to apper dapper appper do," said Abigail eventually.

"Let's go under the roller coaster again. I liked that," said Ernest.

"But the Flyer is so noisy," said Jacob.

"We'll only be there for a minute," said Ernest.

And so from under the roller coaster, the children made their way forward sixty years. It was only when they tumbled out of the laundry basket that they realized they were still wearing the borrowed blazers. The accident of keeping them, if only temporarily,

pleased Abigail, Jacob and Ernest and they folded the blazers up neatly and hid them at the bottom of a laundry basket. They kept the sash there too.

At dinner that evening, their mother told them about the wondrous magic she'd been reading about in *The Enchanted Castle.*

"My new favourite book," she announced.

The children wondered what their mother would think of their adventures and their magic, but they kept silent. They had made a pact.

Abigail put her golden ring under her pillow, next to her autobiography, as yet unfinished.

That night our three children slept contentedly, dreaming of their new friends. And, Simon, Winnifred and Rebecca slept not with contentment, but with hope, as they too dreamt of their new friends.

Chapter Twelve

The Busybody Buddha

February first was Ernest's fifth birthday. In the days leading up to the occasion, Ernest, Jacob and Abigail debated the various ways it could be celebrated.

"Why don't we go back to visit Simon, Winnifred and Rebecca? We could take a picnic with us in the laundry basket and go over to High Park," suggested Jacob.

"I don't know about taking food through time," said Abigail. "You know how concerned Daddy is about bacteria."

"I think food would be all right," said Ernest. "I think Rebecca would like those donuts with all the different coloured sprinkles."

"I don't think we should go to High Park Boulevard for your birthday, Ernest. We'll go another time," said Abigail.

"Why?" asked both brothers.

"Well, they want us to help them, and I'm not sure

we can, and besides which, I don't think we want to celebrate your birthday by feeling responsible to someone else. It's not exactly fun, you know," said Abigail.

"We had fun last time," protested Ernest.

"That's true, but I don't want to go for your birthday. I'd rather go to a foreign country, some place really exotic," said Abigail.

"How are we going to be able to do that?" asked Jacob.

"I don't know. We could borrow some clothes from somebody, or see if we can find something at the Salvation Army," suggested Abigail.

"I want to go into outer space," said Ernest, dreamily.

"Ernest!" cried Abigail and Jacob together.

"There isn't any laundry in space!" continued Jacob.

"You don't know that for sure," said Ernest. "Have you ever been there?"

"I don't want to have this conversation," said Abigail.

"What are we going to do about your birthday, Ernest?" asked Jacob

"I'm thinking," said Ernest.

"I wonder what Mommy and Daddy have planned," said Abigail.

"Mommy will make a Seven-Up cake," said Jacob.

"Beyond that, they probably have no idea," said Abigail. "I want an adventure."

"So do I," agreed Ernest. "I want to see the monkey."

"The monkey in the laundry basket store?" asked Jacob.

"How in the world are we going to get back there?" asked Abigail.

"I think I might just have an idea," said Ernest, and he went up to the playroom to build another fort out of Lincoln Logs.

Abigail went back to writing her autobiography, and Jacob returned to his stack of National Geographics.

"Brian!" cried their mother a few days later. "Brian!" Their father had his headphones on and was playing the guitar along with John Lee Hooker. Abigail jumped up and down in front of him and finally got his attention (he'd had his eyes closed). He took off his headphones, but hung on to his guitar.

"What song are you playing, Daddy?" asked Abigail.

"*Serves Me Right to Suffer*," said her father.

"Is it sad?" asked Jacob.

"It's the blues," said his father.

"Brian, Ernest wants a buddha for his birthday," announced their mother.

"Hmm," said their father, "a buddha? You want that more than some more vehicles or a Winnie the Pooh story tape?"

"I want a buddha," said Ernest.

"And he wants it from the store where we bought the laundry baskets," added their mother.

"I don't think we'll be able to find that place again," said their father.

"We can find it," said Jacob.

"We remember exactly where it was," said Abigail, unconvincingly.

"It's your birthday, Ernest," said their father, putting his headphones back on.

"And we want you to be happy," added their mother.

So, on February first, which was a Saturday, the family once again drove down to Spadina Avenue and, once again, circled Kensington Market for about forty minutes looking for a parking space.

The time spent looking for parking didn't bother the children this time round, since they were trying to get their bearings as to where the shop might be. And

Abigail in particular felt more forgiving of her parents' eccentricities lately.

Something had happened in their laundry travels. The fact that their parents didn't know exactly what to do all the time, or even some of the time, didn't bother her any more. Her experiences on her own had given her the confidence that she could solve problems in the end, even if it didn't feel like that in the middle. She liked being free—laundry magic free—and so did her brothers. Jacob was more confident in his bravery and Ernest was a pretty trustworthy leader (with some exceptions). Their adventures had reassured her about the future. Through their travels they'd also learned that their family didn't lack for love, even though they sometimes lacked direction. Abigail pondered these things as they circled endlessly around Kensington Market.

Everyone was grateful when Jacob, once again, spotted a parking place between a moped (which was completely out of season) and a barrel of herring (which was in season). The parking place was in more or less the same vicinity as the last time they'd visited Kensington Market.

Jacob and Abigail felt anxious as they stepped out of the car: they had no idea which alley (and there were about four right at hand) led to the shop. Their parents stood beside the car, waiting for the children to lead them. No one spoke.

Then, Ernest called out in a clear, bright voice: "It's

me. I'm here. And it's my birthday."

Abigail and Jacob looked at each other in puzzlement and then looked at their parents, who seemed equally puzzled. It was a few moments before anyone noticed Ernest holding a monkey in his arms.

"Whoa!" cried Abigail and Jacob, as if they were reining in a galloping horse.

"Whoa!" echoed their parents, as if grabbing a hold of the same horse.

"This way," said Ernest as he put the monkey (and it was *the* monkey) down and followed it into an alley.

It didn't feel like the same alley to the children or to the parents; there seemed to be a lot more twists and turns this time and no one remembered a big Laundromat next door to the little shop with the beaded curtains. The smell of detergent and bleach was very strong.

Inside, the shop was much the same as before. The Christmas lights gave off the only illumination, and it took a minute or so before everyone could make out the artifacts and objects jumbled throughout the room.

"Ernest!" they all heard a smoky voice call out.

The little old woman from before was standing in a corner, almost hidden in the dark, polishing a buddha.

"It's my birthday," said Ernest.

"So it is," said the woman.

"Ernest wants a buddha for his birthday," explained their mother.

"I have a large selection. Why don't you have a look," said the woman.

"Are they expensive?" asked Abigail.

"Oh, not at all. Go look," the woman said.

Ernest and the monkey were looking through a display case jammed with buddhas: buddhas of different sizes, colours and features, some carved, some cast; no two alike. The monkey chattered at Ernest as Ernest picked up one after another, examining each carefully.

"Don't touch, Ernest," warned their father.

"Let him. He needs to choose," said the woman.

Their mother drifted over to the woks and teapots and cooking utensils. Their father found a pile of maps and started to look through it.

"Do you feel unhappy when it's someone else's birthday?" the woman asked Jacob.

"Not exactly unhappy," said Jacob, "but I like my birthday better."

"I like my birthday the best," said Abigail.

"When I was a little girl, on High Park Boulevard, birthdays were a very formal event," said the woman.

"High Park Boulevard?" asked Jacob as he and Abigail drew in closer to the woman.

The room was so dark, neither Abigail nor Jacob could get a good look at the woman. But they knew right away that she had to be either Winnifred or Rebecca. They had to look into her eyes to tell.

The children had learned in their travels that, through time, everything about a person's appearance might change except the eyes. Deep inside a person's eyes is who they are, maybe even their spirit, and that stays constant.

As if the woman knew what the children were thinking, she flipped on a small desk lamp beside her.

Abigail and Jacob both leaned forward and peered beyond the strawberry hair and the blue, blue eyelids into the deep green eyes before them.

Together they cried out: "Rebecca!"

Ernest and the monkey stopped browsing through the buddhas and Ernest said: "Rebecca?"

The parents paused and looked over to their children, brows furrowed in bewilderment, then they returned to their own browsing.

Ernest moved over to the group. "Jacob wanted to visit you today, and here we are," he said.

"I'm pleased," said Rebecca.

"So, how are you?" asked Jacob.

"As you see me," said Rebecca.

"And Simon and Winnifred?" continued Jacob.

"As good as ever. They're in Peru right now, shopping for the store. Next month all three of us are going to the source of the Nile River," said Rebecca.

"Wow, I'd love to go to the source of the Nile," said Abigail. "Where is it?"

"Far, far away," answered Rebecca. "After we met you three, our taste for adventures grew and grew. But, you'll know all that eventually."

"You mean when we go back to visit you?" asked Jacob.

Rebecca nodded. "Yes."

Ernest moved to stand beside Rebecca, and she put her hand on his shoulder. He looked up at her. "When we go back, do we help you and restore your fortune?"

"Yes and no," she said.

"Rebecca, I have so many questions to ask you," began Jacob. "Like why is Ernest..."

"I don't have any answers, Jacob," Rebecca said this very kindly, but definitively. "You have your own stories."

"Stories?" asked Abigail.

"You mean the books we read?" asked Jacob.

"Your own stories. Books are just the beginning; they'll give you a notion," said Rebecca, picking up the monkey. "A hunch to build on. Your own stories are the maps: your treasure maps. And poems too, poems also help you find your way. There is meaning, always. Now," she said changing the subject, "what about the buddha, Ernest?"

"None of them in the case feels right," said Ernest.

"What did you have in mind?" asked Rebecca.

"I don't know," Ernest replied.

The monkey started to chatter again. It had been quiet for the past few minutes. Rebecca stroked it behind the ears, and it quietened. She picked up the little buddha she'd been polishing when they entered the store and handed it to Ernest. "See what you think of this one. I'm going to check on your parents," and she moved over to the other side of the store, where the children's mother had just decided to buy two wooden ladles, and their father had finally found an interesting map.

Abigail and Jacob huddled with Ernest and the three children stared down at the blue stone figure Ernest held cupped in his hands. Right away, they noticed that it was different from the other buddhas in the shop.

"It looks mischievous," said Jacob.

"More than that," said Abigail.

"This buddha is a busybody," announced Ernest.

"Huh?" said Jacob.

"A busybody buddha. I can feel it," said Ernest.

"Here," demanded Abigail, "let me hold it!"

"No," insisted Ernest, "it's mine!" As he held it firmly in his hands, the little buddha seemed to smile. The children watched it.

"I can feel a story," announced Ernest, "one that no one else knows."

"I don't understand. What's this busybody business?" asked Jacob.

"Someone needs our help," said Ernest.

"Oh no," said Abigail. "If the buddha has to be unusual, why couldn't it grant wishes? Why do we have to help people? It's so ordinary and so...so inconvenient."

No one had an answer to Abigail's questions. The children were quiet.

And then the buddha smiled at them again and they knew: they were on their way to magic and adventures far different from any yet imagined.

Margie Rutledge was born in Midland, Texas. From there she moved steadily north, first to Littleton, Colorado and then on to Calgary, Alberta. As a child she loved to read, particularly in trees. She attended the University of Alberta in Edmonton and graduated with a B.A. in English. Later on she received an M. A. in Drama from the University of Toronto.

Ms Rutledge has worked as a bookstore clerk, a newspaper reporter, and a theatre dramaturge. She currently teaches English as a Second Language and writes newspaper articles, novels and plays. She lives in Toronto with her husband and three children.